# Saving
# Finnegan

Also by Sally Grindley

*Hurricane Wills*
*Spilled Water*
*Feather Wars*

# Saving Finnegan

## Sally Grindley

BLOOMSBURY

First published in Great Britain in 2007 by Bloomsbury Publishing Plc
36 Soho Square, London, W1D 3QY

Copyright © Sally Grindley 2007
The moral right of the author has been asserted

All rights reserved
No part of this publication may be reproduced or transmitted
by any means, electronic, mechanical, photocopying or
otherwise, without the prior permission of the publisher

A CIP catalogue record of this book is available from the British Library

ISBN 978 0 7475 8617 3

All papers used by Bloomsbury Publishing are natural,
recyclable products made from wood grown in well-managed
forests. The manufacturing processes conform to the
environmental regulations of the country of origin.

Typeset by Hewer Text UK Ltd, Edinburgh
Printed in Great Britain by Clays Ltd, St Ives Plc

1 3 5 7 9 10 8 6 4 2

www.bloomsbury.com

*For the Islanders of Coll*

# Chapter 1

Early one morning, before even the cock had crowed, Holly woke up and wondered why. She watched the curtains flapping at her open window. Daylight was just breaking through and chasing the shadows around the room. When a chill draught brushed her face, she pulled Nana Matty's handmade quilt all snuggly round her ears. She closed her eyes and tried to drift back to sleep on the hush of distant waves, but she was too awake and already feeling fidgety.

To stay in bed, or not to stay in bed, that was the question. No one else was up and about, though in the room next door her father was mimicking Gerda the pig with his snorts and grunts and wheezes.

'Oink, oink, oink,' Holly giggled to herself.

What would she do if she got up, she wondered?

She could let the chickens out, but the poxy fox might be lurking in the leftover night, ready to pounce. Poor Miss Marigold, their neighbour, had lost all four of her chickens two weeks before, and she was still in mourning for her poached egg breakfast.

She could make herself a mug of hot chocolate and toast her toes by the kitchen range. Tibbles the cat would be on the comfy chair and would protest pitiably at being dislodged, but she had had it to herself all night, and a cat's place was outdoors catching mice if Holly's father had his way. Which he hadn't, so Tibbles was lucky. Trog the sheepdog wasn't so lucky. A dog's place at night was in his kennel under the stars, and her father did have his way on that, though Trog was quick to flop into his basket in front of the range as soon as the morning door opened and he'd wolfed his biscuits.

Perhaps, Holly thought, I could go down to the beach and skim stones across the silvery sea and watch the sun creeping up on the moon. Or I could run along the sand and frighten the crabs back into their holes.

2

Trog could come with me. He likes chasing crabs because he thinks he can catch them, but he never has and he never will now because his joints are much too rickety.

Not to stay in bed, that was the answer. Holly leapt to her feet, thrusting her quilt on to the creaky old floor, and scuttled to the window to see how far the day had dawned.

The sky was still heavily smeared with inky blue and grey, but patches of golden white and palest blue were stretching out and sweeping them away. From the rooftop, those pesky gulls shrieked their wake-up calls and squabbled over breakfast.

'Yeeek, yeeeek, you're ugly,' Holly yelled up at them. 'Go and find someone else to pester.'

Below, the winding path wove its way from the wobbly back gate of Lobster Pot Cottage, stepped down through the steep grassy slope, shrank past Old Ma Meldrew's (the children called her Mildew) and staggered onwards to the gigantic coal-black rocks that framed the beach.

Holly's eyes stopped on the beach and popped out on stalks.

One of the rocks had been moved!

Instead of forming part of the frame round the beach, this rock was lying as bold as brass right in the middle of the beach.

'Not possible,' Holly muttered to herself. She concentrated her gaze on the displaced rock and tried to conjure up an explanation for its displacement. 'Not possible,' she muttered again.

In the spreading light, Holly began to see that the rock wasn't quite rock-shaped and that it wasn't quite rock-coloured. It was too long and too low and too smooth, and it was browny-grey rather than black. If it's not a rock, then what on earth is it? Holly wondered.

She decided that wondering was all very well, but she wanted to know. She scrambled out of her pyjama bottoms and into her jeans, then pulled Nana Matty's hand-knitted jumper over her pyjama top. She tiptoed across the bedroom, opened the door and listened. Her father's snorts and grunts and wheezes were accompanied now by a gentle whistle. Holly smiled at this alternative dawn chorus as she slipped past her parents' bedroom, on past grotty little George's room, and down the stairs to the front door. She carefully lifted the latch, peered along the road to see if anyone was coming and crept outside.

The sun was rising as she strode round the side of Miss Marigold's cottage and ran to join the winding path. She looked back to see Trog, still head down in his kennel in the back garden, dreaming of crabs.

'Ha, ha,' she chuckled. 'You have failed in your duty to stop an urchin from escaping, O Defender of the Lobster Pot. And I can't take you with me because you'll wake up the whole house, so there.'

She skipped down the steps and slowed by Old Ma Meldrew's.

'I hope the midges are biting,' she mouthed at the blacked-out windows, then stuck her tongue out and scurried on by.

When she reached the rocks, Holly kicked off her trainers and began to climb. At the highest point, she stood up and gazed down across the sand to the alien object.

'What IS it?' she gasped. 'It's HUGE!'

She looked all around her to see if anyone else was about, but though there were lights blinking through the curtains at Curly Lockett's and Jim Robottom's, Holly had the daybreak to herself. She stared again at the brownish-grey, long, smooth object, and an idea began to form in her mind.

'It can't be,' she exclaimed.

She scrambled and slid over the rocks in front of her and began to run across the sand.

'It is!' she cried, clapping her hands. 'It is, it is!'

She stopped, mouth gaping in disbelief. 'Holy mackerel, I've found a whale!' she breathed.

For a moment, Holly didn't know what to do. She thought about racing home and fetching her father and mother, but if she went away someone else might find her whale and steal it from her.

Then she thought she heard the whale sigh.

She ran a few steps towards it, but stopped in her tracks when it groaned loudly, shuddered and thrashed its huge tail.

'Eek!' she cried. It dawned on her that this was no puppy she was about to go and comfort. This was the biggest beast she had ever seen in her life, a hundred times as big as an elephant even. It might be dangerous. It might eat her! One slip into its enormous

6

mouth (if it opened it) and she would be like Jonah. She might never see her father and mother and Nana Matty and Tibbles and Trog again. (She didn't mind so much about George.) And then she thought, it hasn't got legs so it can't run after me. The best it can do is flump, and I'm sure I can run a lot faster than it can flump.

She crept towards it, worried that it might be frightened. She could see its great chest heaving and its tiny half-closed eyes. She was worried then that it might be ill.

'Don't die, Mr Whale,' she whispered. 'Please don't die.'

The whale shuddered again and swept its tail slowly, sadly Holly thought, backwards and forwards across the wet sand. Holly looked towards the sea, which was rolling further and further away into the horizon.

'It'll come back to fetch you later on,' she said, 'if you can just be patient.'

The whale seemed to sigh again, a tremble of air escaping from its blowhole. Holly wished she could go closer and put her arms round its neck, but she didn't dare. She wanted someone to come now, someone who would know what to do. She gazed back at the village, ready to pounce upon anything that moved (as long as it wasn't Old Ma Meldrew). There were lights on in more of the cottages. There was a light on downstairs in Lobster Pot Cottage, but the curtains were still closed. Dad, Holly thought, making Mum her cup of tea to prise her out of bed. Dad, yawning under his sticky-up hair, mooching around in his slippers. Dad, having a bit of quiet time before opening the door to Trog with his wagging tail and his are-you-pleased-to-see-me eyes.

'Open the door now,' Holly willed him. 'I need you, Dad.'

A movement on the road up to the right of the cottages caught her eye. The postman's van. It came down towards their cottage then disappeared behind it. It seemed to stay there for ever.

'Stop gossiping,' Holly muttered. 'I bet they're going on about fish, fish, fish.'

At last the van reappeared round the other side of the cottage, heading towards the back of the beach. Holly jumped up and down and waved her arms wildly above her head. She giggled when the whale thrashed its tail as well.

'Postie,' she yelled. 'Come here, quickly. It's a whale, Postman Cyril. I've found a whale!'

# Chapter 2

If she could have shared the discovery of her whale with someone other than Postman Cyril Blackburn, Holly would certainly have done so. She didn't like him very much. Neither did many of the village children. He had a knobbly, purple, strawberry-shaped nose, which he poked into other people's business. Mum said it was caused by an unhealthy fondness for moonshine. Holly laughed when she said that, and told her that she'd got her shines wrong.

'It's sunshine you've got to be careful of,' she giggled.

Mum had winked at Dad. 'Don't you be so sure,' she smiled.

Another thing about Postman Cyril was that he had killer bad breath. He could blast a hole through a brick wall at fifty paces, her friend Freddy Roberts calculated.

You had to keep far enough away from him, or wear a mask, to survive.

Holly had no choice but to seek his help, because there was nobody else around. As soon as he heaved himself from his van outside the village shop, she leapt up and down again.

'Postman Cyril, come quickly,' she called out. 'I need your help.'

The postman turned to look at her, but was about to continue on his round when he saw that there was something unusual on the beach and headed in her direction instead.

'What have you been up to, young lady?' he shouted as he puffed his way down the winding path. 'Does your father know you're out?' Holly raised her eyes to heaven and imagined him buried up to his neck in the sand with crabs pinching his purple nose. He vanished behind the rocks and she waited impatiently until he reappeared on top.

'What's that you've got there then?' he wheezed, wiping the steam from his glasses.

What do you think it is? Holly thought. 'It's a whale, Postie. I've found a whale,' she said.

11

The postman slithered and slid and stumbled over the rocks in front of him and waddled over to Holly.

'Well I never, so it is,' he puffed. 'What's it doing there then?'

'It must have got stuck here when the tide went out,' she offered. 'What do you think we should do, Postie?'

He moved closer to the whale, bent over and peered at its half-closed eyes.

'I should think it wants a bit of water,' he said. 'Have you got a bucket with you?'

I'm not a baby, Holly sighed to herself. 'A bucket's like a thimble to a whale that size,' she said. 'Anyway, the sea's too far away. What about a hose?'

'A hose, that's a good idea,' agreed the postman. 'You go and fetch one while I stay here and look after it.'

Holly looked daggers at him. 'It's my whale. You should fetch the hose while I look after it.'

'Now don't you be silly, young lady,' he argued. 'Your legs are much younger than mine.'

Holly was about to answer back when to her enormous relief she saw the back door of Lobster Pot Cottage open. Her father came out and Trog went berserk, blundering round and round him on his rickety legs and barking riotously. Holly leapt up and down and shouted until she was hoarse, but her father didn't hear her above Trog's racket. He was about to turn back into the house, when Trog spotted her and launched himself in her direction, at least as far as the gate. He stood there howling to be let loose. Her father looked up as he tried to shoo him indoors but failed to budge him. Holly waved her arms and leapt and shrieked and shouted.

'You'll frighten the poor beast to death,' Postman Cyril said behind her.

You could asphyxiate the poor beast, Holly thought to herself.

Her father was through the gate now and on his way down the path at breakneck speed. When at last his head popped up above the top of the rocks, he called down, 'What on earth are you doing out here, Holly? You're supposed to be in bed.'

'It's a whale, Dad. I found it. It needs some water badly.'

Her father scrambled across the rocks and jogged over to her.

'It's in a bit of a bad way, I'd say,' said the postman.

Her father moved closer to the whale and bent over it. It flapped its tail limply.

'It'll be all right, won't it, Dad?' Holly asked anxiously.

'I'm no expert, sunshine,' he replied, 'but I'm sure we need to get it some water, and quickly.'

'Can it be mine though, Dad?' Holly grabbed his elbow as he straightened up.

'We haven't got a pond,' he grinned and began to march away. 'I'm off to fetch the fire brigade. It'll give Danny Perkins something to keep himself occupied. And I'll bring the vet as well.'

Holly swiped at her father as he strode by. 'I meant can I be in charge of it because I found it,' she said urgently.

'I'm sure Cyril will want to carry on with his round,' he smiled. 'He can let everyone know what you've discovered and bring more help.'

'Of course,' said the postman quickly. 'I'll be getting off then.'

He waddled away across the sand, puffing in her father's wake.

Left to herself, Holly sat down a few feet from the whale and talked gently to it about anything she could think of. The sun was shining brightly now, lighting sparklers along the horizon where it met the sea. It was going to be hot again, even though it was the beginning of autumn. Holly wanted it to stay hot because she liked to be outside.

'Mum says I'm a tomboy, which is a bit true, but sometimes I want to surprise everybody and turn into a princess, just like a caterpillar turns into a beautiful butterfly.'

Her mother didn't like it hot. It made her hair go frizzy, she said. It made her brain perspire and her feet balloon. It made the butter melt, but if you kept it in the fridge it turned into a brick. Her mother didn't like the rain either. It made her hair go lank, she said. It pitter-pattered on the lean-to roof and splattered from the gutters until it made her teeth go tight.

'You'd like it wet rather than hot, wouldn't you, poor old thing?' Holly said to the whale.

Her mother liked it not too hot and not too cold and not too windy and only wet in the night when she was fast asleep.

'She's a bit fussy I think,' observed Holly out loud. 'But all grown-ups are fussy in one way or another. It's something that just happens to you when you get older. I won't let it happen to me. Dad's fussy about his fishing nets and his vegetables and his CD collection, and he doesn't like people who poke their noses into his business, which Postman Cyril does, people who suck their teeth, oh and he doesn't like beetroot.'

The whale gave a great shudder, which Holly took to mean that it didn't like beetroot either. She wondered suddenly whether it was a male or a female. How could you tell? She chuckled when she thought that the only way to find out might be to roll it over.

'I think you're probably a boy,' she said, 'because you're so enormous.'

She decided that she should give it a name before anyone else came along and called it something stupid like Nigel or Big Boy or Tiddler. She tried out lots of different names, quietly so as not to offend the whale, but nothing sounded right. Then, out of the corner of her eye, she spotted something moving at the top of the rocks. She looked up and saw George, followed by her mother.

'Oh no! Why did you go and tell them, Dad?' she muttered to herself.

There was no way she was going to allow her little brother to name the whale. She looked at the enormous creature and the neat fin on its back.

'Finnegan,' she said out loud. 'That's what your name is – Finnegan.'

'WOW!' she heard George exclaim. 'Look how big it is, Mummy!'

'I found it. It's my whale,' Holly yelled. 'It's called Finnegan.'

'Who says?' said George as he ran across the sand towards her. 'That's a silly name.'

'Who cares what you think?' Holly snapped.

Her mother padded up to them, warning them not to go any closer to the stranded animal.

'It might be dangerous,' she said. 'Animals can be very unpredictable when they're in trouble. What are you doing out here anyway, Holly?'

'Couldn't sleep,' Holly replied, feeling peevish that she was being told what to do when it was her whale and she had been looking after him for ages while everyone else played lazybones in bed.

'It looks dead,' said George.

'He's not dead,' retorted Holly. 'I've been talking

to him and he's waved his tail and sighed. But he needs some water to keep him cool until the tide comes in.'

'Can't he just scrabble and slide back to the sea? That's what seals do, I've seen it on the telly,' said George.

Holly looked at her mother and raised her eyes heavenwards.

'He's not a seal,' she said scornfully.

'He's too heavy to move without the water, love,' said their mother.

'Has he got teeth?' asked George, kneeling down in the sand for a closer look.

'Yes, and he's going to eat you all up!' shrieked Holly. She threw herself on top of her brother and tickled him until he screamed for mercy. The whale groaned loudly and thrashed its tail, which stopped Holly and her brother in mid-tickle.

'Not all whales have teeth,' said their mother. 'Blue whales don't and they're the biggest of the lot.'

'Is Finnegan a blue whale?' asked Holly.

As she spoke, they heard voices and saw a group of villagers, laden with buckets, making their way through the opening at the back of the beach and across the sand.

Holly prepared to confront them with her right of ownership, just in case any of them thought they could take charge over a slip of a girl.

'He's called Finnegan and I found him and he's not to be upset,' she cried out to the first in line, which was Big Jim Robottom in his big black wellington boots.

'Morning, Jim,' said her mother. 'You're the only one carrying two buckets and you're still the winner. What do you think of your prize?'

Holly liked Big Jim, the ferryman who took people backwards and forwards to the mainland and helped carry their shopping. He was a gentle giant with a twinkle in his eyes and and a big black stubbly beard like a pirate might have. When he danced at the Christmas ceilidh in the Big Old Barn, all tread-on-your-toes and boompsadaisy, her mother said it was just as well there weren't any floorboards because he would catapult them in the air.

'He's a whopper,' Big Jim admired. 'He must have taken some catching.'

'He's a WHOPPER!' shrieked George, stretching out his arms as far as they would go.

Holly was about to explain patiently to Big Jim that she hadn't caught the whale, when she saw him wink at her mother.

'Where would you like the water, miss?' he continued playfully.

'Head, first, I think,' said Holly seriously. 'And don't get too close because animals can be very unpredictable when they're in trouble.'

'Of course, miss. Anything you say, miss.'

He bowed and picked up his two buckets all in one movement. As he strode towards the whale, he turned to say, 'Don't let anyone throw water into his blowhole. He breathes through that, you know.'

Holly didn't know, but she nodded as if she did. Big Jim stood as close to the whale as he dared, then lifted one bucket at a time and launched the water over the front of the whale's head, to George's excited cries of 'SPLASH!' The whale shuddered and its tail jerked. George launched himself on to the sand and wriggled and squiggled and squealed.

'If you're not careful,' warned their mother, 'we'll send the next bucket of water over *your* head.'

'You wouldn't dare,' shrieked George.

'*I* would,' said Holly.

By now more villagers had struggled over with their buckets and were awaiting instructions, all except Councillor Reginald Hodson. He was giving instructions, even though he hadn't brought a bucket. Holly narrowed her eyes at him. Typical, she thought. Trust you to think you should take charge. She imagined him as a toad, with his fat, wrinkly face and Humpty-Dumpty body.

'Crawl back under your stone,' she muttered. Then, out loud for everyone to hear, she announced, 'My whale's name is Finnegan and nobody must throw water into his blowhole because that's how he breathes.'

She was relieved when Big Jim offered to be the chief water launcher until Danny Perkins, the fireman, arrived. Councillor Hodson told people to stand in line ready to hand over their bucket, and then plodded closer to have a look at the whale. He was inspecting the tail end, when Big Jim launched another bucketful of water. The whale thrashed its tail wildly, which caused the alarmed Councillor to lose his balance and topple over backwards in the sand. A hysterical hoot escaped from

Holly's lips. Her mother nudged her sharply in the ribs, while the other villagers gasped and George threw himself backwards into the sand.

'That made you jump,' Holly smirked. (Except that toads don't jump, she thought, they crawl.)

'Not at all,' spluttered Councillor Hodson as he struggled to his feet and brushed himself down. 'Lost my footing, that's all.'

'It might be safer not to go too close,' Big Jim suggested, winking at Holly.

'That's all very well,' huffed the Councillor, 'but we need some proper advice about how to deal with this beast. We can't just leave it here.'

'I don't think we have much choice until the tide comes back in,' said Big Jim.

'Well, I shall go and ring the mainland and see what they think.'

'Dad's fetching Mrs Roberts,' Holly informed him.

'I hardly think our vet will know what to do,' scoffed the Councillor. 'It's not as if she has a whale to deal with every day.'

He turned and trudged back up the beach. Holly was delighted to see that he had a round wet patch on the back of his trousers from when he had fallen.

'Can't trust us to deal with the problem ourselves, can he?' grumbled Curly Lockett who, with his wife, provided a taxi service for the islanders. 'Always has to check with the mainland.'

'Aye, that's right,' grimaced Betty Lockett. 'Like we're a bunch of dimwits.'

'I expect he just thinks he's doing his job,' Holly's mother observed, always the one to try and keep the peace.

'Doing his job my foot,' joined in Jean Westcott, the landlady of the village pub. 'Licking the boots of authority more like.'

'Yuck!' said George.

'Well, unless any of us here is an expert on whales, then we need someone to tell us how best to keep this poor thing alive,' Holly's mother continued, and everyone went very quiet.

A loud siren broke the silence. At the far end of the beach, where the road ran down to a gap in the rocks, Danny Perkins's shiny engine, freed for once from its shed, hurtled towards them. Its blue light swept large circles round and round the beach.

'That's enough to frighten our whale to death and wake up the entire island,' said Big Jim.

The fire engine slewed to a halt a few yards from them. Fireman Perkins jumped down from his cab, followed by Holly's father and the vet, Mrs Roberts, her friend Freddy's mother.

'Well,' exclaimed Danny Perkins, 'I've had to deal with some strange things in my time, but this beats the lot!'

'His name's Finnegan, and I found him,' said Holly. 'He needs water badly.'

'I'd better get the hose on him then,' said the fireman. He went to the side of the fire engine and began to detach the hose, while Patricia Roberts went towards the whale.

'Be careful,' said Holly. 'Animals can be unpredictable when they're in trouble.'

'I'll be careful,' the vet smiled.

'What are you going to do?' asked Holly.

'I need to check how stressed he is,' the vet replied. 'This is quite an ordeal for him.'

Holly wondered how you could tell if a whale was stressed. 'He will be all right, won't he?' she asked. 'He's been moving his tail.'

The vet smiled a tight sort of smile. 'Only time will tell,' she said.

She squatted down by the whale's side and began to examine the creature carefully. Holly watched in anxious silence, along with the other villagers, whose numbers were swelling by the minute.

As soon as she had finished, Mrs Roberts signalled to Danny Perkins that he should start to spray the whale.

'Can I hold the hose?' George pleaded.

'No you can't,' huffed Holly, before Danny Perkins had a chance to answer.

'It's a bit heavy for you, lad.'

Nevertheless, George hung on to the hose halfway down as the fireman pulled the nozzle towards the whale. Holly growled and looked to her father for support, but he was talking with Big Jim, and her mother was surrounded by the other villagers.

'Mind you don't squirt water into his blowhole,' Holly said sharply when Danny Perkins took aim.

A huge fountain of water shot up into the air and showered down on the whale. The whale shuddered and groaned, silencing the chattering crowd. George let go of the hose and ran to dance in the spray. He shrieked loudly.

'Stop him, Mum,' Holly cried. 'He'll upset my whale.'

'George, come here this minute,' her mother shouted.

George carried on his dance, until Constable Brenda McKee, the village police officer, pushed her way forward through the crowd and began to order people to move right away from the whale. Holly's father grabbed her brother round the waist and carried him protesting to his mother's side.

'Pain, isn't he?' a voice behind Holly said.

She turned to find Freddy Roberts.

'In the butt,' she grimaced.

'It's amazing to think something that big can float when it's in the sea,' he said.

'I presume you mean my whale and not George,' Holly grinned.

She liked Freddy. He was sporty and no-nonsense and didn't always do what he was told. He was the tallest in her class, had thick black curly hair, an earring in one ear (much to the horror of some of the older islanders) and holes in his jeans which showed a tiny bit of his thigh. He wasn't silly or irritating like most of the boys of her age, and he challenged the teachers if he thought they were talking rubbish – which sometimes they were. Freddy was an expert on anything to do with the sea and the tides and the moon. It was his passion and he was quick to correct anyone who got things wrong.

'It could be ill,' he said. 'Mum said sometimes whales beach if their navigation system is affected by illness.'

Holly gazed at him. She didn't want her whale to be ill. 'He could just have been caught up with the tide,' she said.

'Unlikely,' replied Freddy, 'though why whales beach is all still a bit of a mystery.'

Just then the school bell rang, taking everyone by surprise. Holly's father told her to run there quickly and that he hadn't realised it was so late, while her mother tussled with George, who was having a tantrum. Holly didn't want to go to school. Looking after her whale was much more important than geometry or grammar or levers.

'I haven't had any breakfast yet, and I need to get changed for school, and I want to stay with my whale,' she answered back.

'School's important,' her father said, 'and your whale will still be here when you finish.'

'Real life's important,' argued Holly, but she knew she wasn't going to win.

She trailed along with Freddy, back across the beach and over the rocks, looking over her shoulder every few steps to see what the adults were up to.

'It's not fair,' she growled. 'Why should they have all the fun?'

'It's not going to be that much fun, standing on the beach all day watching them spray water over the poor thing.'

'Still better than listening to Mrs Hardaway droning on.'

# Chapter 3

Holly stopped off at Lobster Pot Cottage to change her clothes and snatch something to eat. Trog was in the kitchen, indignant at being left behind when there was clearly something of interest going on outside, especially since it meant that he hadn't yet had his breakfast. He fussed around Holly's feet until she shouted at him to leave her in peace.

'It's bad enough that they've stolen my whale, without your pestering,' she stormed, but she felt guilty when she saw the puzzlement in Trog's eyes, and threw some biscuits into his bowl. She tore herself a large chunk of bread, cut a sizeable hunk of cheese, and slammed out of the front door.

The road that ran past the cottage meandered gently

along the coastline for a few hundred yards, before twisting sharply away from the sea, almost doubling back on itself, and then climbing upwards towards the island's only hotel. Beyond that, it passed by another group of cottages before diverting briefly through the gates of the village school, and then continued past the village hall and through moorland to the next bay. Looking up, Holly could see a straggle of latecomers plunging through the gates and into the school building. If she had felt like it, she could have cut straight up through the grass and on to the road where it passed above the cottage, instead of following it all the way round. She didn't feel like it though. She wanted to keep an eye on what was happening on the beach.

As she dawdled along, she saw that several of the villagers had tired already of whale-watching and were making their way back across the rocks. Others stood in clumps talking as only adults could.

'Yak, yak, yak,' Holly muttered to herself, dragging her feet on the cracked tarmac.

'You'll ruin your shoes, young lady,' a voice scolded from somewhere below. Holly looked down to see Old Ma Meldrew hanging out her washing.

'How can you worry about washing when there's a whale on the beach?' she retorted.

'There's plenty enough people worrying about that whale without it needing me to interfere,' she snorted.

Holly was about to say something else when her mother appeared on the path below, pulling a sodden George behind her.

'Will you get a move on, Holly,' she ordered. 'You're already late.'

'So's George,' said Holly.

'Don't answer back,' her mother snapped. 'George isn't going anywhere without a change of clothes.'

'I want to stay with the whale,' George wailed.

'If I can't, you can't.' Holly flung her words at him.

'All this fuss about a whale,' sniffed Old Ma Meldrew.

'Yeah, like it happens every day,' muttered Holly.

However hard she tried, Holly could not find a nice thought to think about her, even though she knew from her mother that Old Ma Meldrew had had a difficult life. She was such a killjoy she didn't even go to the Christmas ceilidh. She refused to go near it, calling it the devil's playground and anyone attending the devil's servants.

Holly strode away from her. Down on the beach, she could see Danny Perkins, Big Jim and her father by the whale, deep in conversation. Heading towards them was Councillor Hodson. Holly wondered if he had been able to get through to the mainland this early in the morning, and harboured thoughts of bringing down the telephone lines so that he wouldn't be able to. He was just like Mary Cooper in her class, always telling tales and sucking up to teacher. She knew her father didn't like him. It was his fault that he had had a speeding fine, which put him in a bad mood for days. There were no speed limits on their island until Councillor Hodson had suggested to their local authority on the mainland that it would be a good idea. The islanders had been furious when the council sent over gangs of surly road main-tenance workers, not to repair the disintegrating road surfaces, but to put up lollipop signs telling them to slow down or not to exceed a certain speed. Holly's father said he could walk faster than the speed at which he was now supposed to drive his car, and that in any case you couldn't go too fast on the island roads. They were so full of bumps and bends and potholes and cracks, you'd be more likely to have a heart attack than to crash.

Holly rounded the bend and began the steep climb up towards the school. There were no other children in sight now, and she knew she would be in trouble for being late.

'I'm sorry I'm late, miss,' she rehearsed, 'but I was distracted by a whale.' And, 'I'm whaley sorry I'm late, miss.' And, 'I'm sorry I'm late but I've been having a whale of a time.'

She giggled to herself, then took one last look behind her at the beach and her whale before it disappeared from sight.

'Take care, Finnegan,' she breathed. 'I'll come and see you later.'

She crossed the playground and tiptoed through the front door. She didn't want Mr Rowland, the Head-teacher, to see her. It was one thing being in trouble with Mrs Hardaway. It was quite another to be in trouble with Mr Rowland. It wasn't that he was fright-ening. In fact, he was quite a friendly character as headteachers go. It was more that he was very good at dreaming up embarrassing or tedious punishments if you did something wrong. Once, when Freddy was late, he had made him sweep up all the leaves in the playground, even though it was the windiest day of the year and every time he swept them into a pile they blew away again. Another time he had made Alfie Perkins serve the brussels sprouts at lunchtime, with the instruction that he pile them high on every plate regardless of any protests.

She made it to her classroom door, knocked, swung into the room quickly, and slammed the door behind her. When she turned round, she came face to face with Mr Rowland.

'Ah, Holly Wainwright,' he beamed, peering at her over the top of his spectacles, 'how nice of you to join us.'

'It's nice to be here, sir,' said Holly, trying to compose herself. 'I'm sorry I'm late, but there was this whale on the beach and I found it and I've been looking after it, sir.'

'Yes, we know all about the whale,' he said. 'In fact, I was just saying to Mrs Hardaway that she should take your class down to see it, and I shall call on it later on. After all, it's not every day we have an opportunity to make the acquaintance of a whale.'

'No, sir,' said Holly. 'That's just what I think.'

'Of course,' said the Head, 'there'll be no need for you to go since you've already, by your own account, "been looking after it", so you can stay here and sharpen all the pencils in the stationery cupboard.'

'But that's not fair, sir,' protested Holly, while the rest of the class tittered.

'And it's not fair of you to turn up after Mrs Hardaway has started her lesson,' he said, and turned to leave. As he reached the door, he turned back and smiled at Holly. 'So that we don't waste this opportunity to enlighten ourselves about the life and habits of such a whale, when you've finished sharpening the pencils, you can look it up on the internet and tell us all about it.'

Holly wanted to scream. Here she was being told to sharpen pencils instead of going to see her whale, and yet at the same time she was being asked to find out all about him. She could find out more, she thought, if she were allowed to spend more time with him. She flumped down at her desk and pretended to listen to what Mrs Hardaway was saying, but she couldn't see the point of decimal fractions at the best of times, and she certainly couldn't be bothered with them now.

When Mrs Hardaway had her back to them, Alice

Hodson, who sat across the aisle from her, leant over and whispered, 'That whale might die.'

'Not if I can help to save him,' Holly whispered back.

'How will you do that if you're going to be stuck in the cupboard?' Alice snorted.

'Funny ha ha,' Holly hissed. She wasn't in the mood for Alice and her buck teeth and ponytail, especially not on top of pencil sharpening and decimal fractions. Besides, she didn't want to think about the possibility that her whale might die. She was sure that if she could just go and sit with him and talk to him, he would be all right until the tide came to fetch him.

'I saw the whale from my bedroom window, but Mummy wouldn't let me go down to the beach in case it was dangerous,' Alice continued.

Holly wondered if Alice was challenging her ownership of the whale. 'I saw it even before it was daylight,' she said, 'and I went and talked to it while everyone else was asleep.'

'You're lucky it didn't eat you,' Alice taunted.

'I hope it eats you,' Holly bristled, then saw that Mrs Hardaway was hovering by her desk.

Mrs Hardaway had a long, thin body topped with a

mass of tangled hair, like candyfloss on a stick, except that her hair was bright ginger. She wore lashings of black mascara, which made her look rather startled, and burnt orange lipstick, which made her look as if she'd been at the marmalade. Holly's father said that you can't always judge a present by its wrapping, and that Daphne Hardaway was full of fun and nonsense, and soft as butter.

Holly couldn't imagine it as Mrs Hardaway towered over her now.

'Am I boring you today, Holly? Not that I've had much opportunity given how late you arrived.'

'No, Mrs Hardaway, you're not boring me at all,' Holly replied. 'I love decimal fractions.'

'Then kindly show your enjoyment by paying some attention, or I shall set you a sheet of them for homework.'

Holly ignored Alice's grin of triumph and tried hard to concentrate. The last thing she wanted was homework, especially when Finnegan needed her.

When the bell went for the end of the lesson, Mrs Hardaway asked the rest of the class to leave their things neatly on their desks and line up ready to walk down to the beach. As they filed noisily through the door and along the corridor to the main entrance, she told Holly to make her way to the stationery cupboard and then added quietly, 'Don't worry, Holly. We'll make sure your whale's all right.'

From the tiny stationery cupboard window, Holly watched her classmates rolling uproariously down the road until they disappeared from sight. She toyed with the idea of sneaking after them, like a secret agent tracking the enemy, but she knew the Head might check up on her and she didn't want to risk incurring more of his inventive punishments. She looked round for the pencils. There were boxloads of them, coloured and plain-leaded, at least half of them as blunt as the nose of a Persian kitten. The only pencil sharpener she could find was the old sort – small, silver and not very sharp – not one of those modern ones where you stick the pencil in a hole, wait for the whirr, then whisk it out all sharp as a compass point.

'Trust this place not to have a decent sharpener,' Holly muttered.

She picked up a box of lead pencils, took it back to her classroom, sat down and began sharpening. By the time she'd finished a third box, her fingers were aching and shiny black.

'I refuse to do any more,' she said out loud, just as Mr Rowland walked through the door.

'Ah, Holly,' he said, 'and how's it going?'

'My fingers have dropped off, sir,' groaned Holly, trying to sound as forlorn as possible.

'That's a shame, because you'll need them to look up your whale on the internet,' said the Head, raising his eyebrows above his spectacles.

'Oh, I think I can just about manage that, sir, despite the pain,' Holly said quickly.

'Well, let's hope you can remember enough about the whale to be able to identify it,' the Head smiled as he left the room.

'Doh! Of course I can remember,' Holly muttered. She washed her hands in the corner sink, then sat herself down at the classroom computer.

She typed WHALE into the search engine and waited for the web addresses to appear. There was no broad-band on the island, so it took ages, and then it took ages again when she pounced on a site that promised to list all whale species, with descriptions and photographs.

At last the screen opened up. Holly ignored the paragraph that discussed whales in general and scanned through the list of species. She knew the blue whale was the biggest, and Finnegan was certainly big, so she scrolled down to that first. But when she read the description, she realised that her whale was the wrong colour for him to be a blue whale. She went back a page and scanned the list again. She thought she was seeing things when suddenly the name FIN WHALE sprang out at her.

'Is that what Finnegan is?' she wondered out loud.

She clicked on the name and waited impatiently for information about the whale to appear. It seemed to take longer than ever and Holly felt like kicking the computer to make it go faster.

At last a photograph of the fin whale filled the screen. Holly gazed at it intently, read the accompanying description, then leapt to her feet. She hurtled out of the classroom, down the corridor, knocked on Mr Rowland's door and barged in before he could answer.

'I've found it, sir,' she cried excitedly. 'You'll never believe it, but it's called a fin whale. And I named him *Finn*egan!'

The Head looked at her sceptically. 'What a coincidence! I've never heard of a fin whale before.'

'A fin whale is the second largest whale next to the blue whale, which makes it the second largest animal on earth. Imagine that, sir – we've got the second largest animal on earth on our beach!'

'Impressive,' said Mr Rowland.

'It's a fast swimmer and is sometimes called "the greyhound of the sea" because of its speed.'

'Ours isn't moving very fast,' joked the Head.

'Sir,' protested Holly, 'you're not taking this seriously.'

'I do apologise, Holly,' he said. 'Do carry on.'

Holly looked at him crossly before continuing. 'It's dark grey-brown or black on top and white underneath – which is just like my whale. It's got two blowholes, and it feeds on plankton and other small sea creatures – not humans.'

'I shouldn't think it comes across a human in the normal course of things,' Mr Rowland smiled.

Holly glared at him witheringly. He might think he was being funny, but she did not.

'Well done, Holly,' he said. 'As soon as everyone has

returned, I shall ask you to tell them what you've discovered.'

Holly went back to the classroom to wait. Outside the sky was a brilliant blue, broken only by the slightest smudges of cloud. It was the sort of day when nobody should have to be indoors, Holly thought, and especially not in boring old school doing boring things like sharpening pencils. The sun was pounding through the windows and bleaching the colour from the art-works which decorated the walls. Holly threw the windows open and breathed in the fresh morning air. Then she went to the art cupboard, took out a handful of colouring pencils and a large piece of paper, and sat down to draw her whale.

She had just put the finishing touches to her whale's face and was writing the name 'Finnegan' in bold red letters underneath, when she heard shrill voices. She didn't really want to be there when her classmates came back into the classroom. She didn't want to hear them boasting about what they'd been doing. She didn't want to hear them talking about her whale. She put her drawing in her desk and returned the pencils to the cupboard. Quickly, she sat herself down at the computer and logged into a race game. The first of her classmates crashed through the door.

'Cor, can I play?' said Alfie Perkins.

'You're supposed to be sharpening pencils,' said Mary Cooper.

'My dad says it's probably not worth trying to save that whale,' said Alice Hodson.

'It's the biggest, hugest, enormousest thing I've ever seen in my life,' said Benjamin Westcott. 'It makes my dad look like an ant.'

'It makes my dad look like a flea,' said Susie Tyler.

'My mum says it's a blue whale,' said Marjorie Daws.

'It is NOT a blue whale,' said Holly loudly, jumping to her feet. 'It's a FIN whale.'

There was a moment of silence while her classmates took this in, then several of them began to titter.

'There's no such thing as a fin whale,' sniggered Marjorie Daws.

A loud voice from the doorway called the chattering class to attention.

'Holly is quite right,' boomed the Head, 'and if you would all like to sit down at your desks like civilised human beings, then she will be happy to enlighten you.'

Everyone shuffled sheepishly to their seats, while Mrs Hardaway regained authority from the front of the class. She called Holly to stand next to her and waited for silence. Holly wasn't sure she wanted to enlighten her classmates. Let them think Finnegan was a blue whale if they wanted – she didn't care, especially if they were going to make fun of her because of its name. But they were all sitting watching her now, and she had no choice but to tell them what she had found out.

As soon as she had finished, she leapt down from the platform and plonked herself down at her desk.

'Well done, Holly,' said Mrs Hardaway. 'I'm sure your prompt action in raising the alarm will have helped your whale's chances of surviving.'

'And she named it Finnegan,' said Freddy.

'Very appropriate,' Mrs Hardaway nodded.

'Doesn't mean it's your whale,' Alice leant across and whispered.

'What's it like being ugly?' Holly muttered back.

'For the rest of the morning,' Mrs Hardaway continued, 'I want you either to paint a fully labelled picture of a whale, or to write a story about a whale.'

'Can I do both?' asked Mary.

Holly groaned. If only this day would end and she could go home.

# Chapter 4

When, at last, the bell rang for the end of the day, Holly made a dash for the classroom door and ran from the school house as quickly as she could, earning the rebuke 'Walk, don't run' as she shot past the Head. Before she had gone very far, she heard a voice behind her calling for her to wait.

Freddy puffed up level with her. 'You going down there?' he asked.

'Course,' said Holly, pleased that it was Freddy and not one of her other classmates. 'The tide will be in soon and I want to watch Finnegan swim away.'

'You know they think he's probably going to die,' he said quietly, thrusting his hands in his pockets and looking at the ground.

Holly felt her eyes pricking. 'They can't know that,' she said mutinously. 'They didn't even know what sort of whale he is.'

'When we were down there earlier, Piggy Hodson came back from talking to the mainland. He said Mum was right and that the most likely reason for a whale to beach is illness.'

'He could get better,' insisted Holly.

'Might be best to expect the worst,' Freddy suggested.

'Might be best to be optimistic,' countered Holly.

They hurried on down the road, Holly trying to blot out any thought that Finnegan might not survive. It was such a beautiful day. The afternoon sun cast an amber glow across the bay, but at the same time it blackened the rocks so that they surrounded the beach like a huge cloak of doom, dwarfing the whale. The fire engine was still stationed on the sand, and row upon row of islanders were pressing for a closer look from behind a line of plastic barriers. Constable McKee was marching up and down trying to keep order.

'Where have all those people come from?' Holly asked in astonishment.

'Word's got round across the island, I expect,' said

Freddy. 'They all want to see the whale before he goes away.'

'Shall we watch from the rocks? We'll see better from there.'

'Could do, but we might not be allowed with the tide coming in. Nobody else is there.'

'It's never stopped us before. Come on,' said Holly defiantly.

They ran on down the road. When they reached Lobster Pot Cottage, Holly peered through the windows to check if anyone was in. She could see her mother, silhouetted against the rear kitchen window, pounding away at a stretch of dough. Through another window, she could see George glued to the television. The infants finished school two hours earlier than she did. He was watching cartoons and had obviously forgotten about the real live whale on the beach. He turned in her direction and she ducked down below the windowsill, pulling Freddy away as she did.

'Don't let him see you,' she hissed. 'He'll want to come with us.'

They crawled along the pavement until they reached the side of the house, then made a dash to the path.

'I hope all the other kids don't come,' Holly said as they headed for the rocks, which looked much less hostile now they were close to them.

'You can't stop them,' Freddy grinned.

'Worse luck,' said Holly. 'I wish it was like early this morning, just me and Finnegan.'

'Thanks!' said Freddy.

He launched himself at the rocks, pulling athletically with his hands and feet, and reached the top before Holly had even scrabbled up on to the first level. When she hauled herself up alongside him, catching hold of his hand to steady herself, she felt as if they were the most important people on the whole island. They had been singled out to share this extraordinary spectacle from the best seat in the house.

She screwed up her eyes to see if she could spot her father, and was disappointed to discover that he wasn't there. Didn't he care enough? Big Jim, Mrs Roberts and Danny Perkins were standing close to the whale, but so was Councillor Hodson. Hadn't he got any work to do?

The sea rolled in and spilled over the sand only a few inches away from the whale's tail. One large wave and Finnegan would feel its heavenly pull.

'The sea's nearly there, Freddy,' she said excitedly.

She called out to Big Jim, but he didn't hear her above the rush of the sea and the hubbub of the crowd. Freddy's mother waved at them, and as they waved back they saw that someone else was waving urgently in their direction.

'I don't think we're supposed to be here,' said Freddy.

Constable McKee was marching towards them, signalling for them to come down from the rocks.

'You can't stay there,' they heard her shout as she drew nearer. 'We can't have you climbing about on the rocks when the tide's coming in, not with all these people around.'

'But we come up here all the time,' Holly shouted back.

'Yes, I know you do,' the Constable replied, 'but if I let you stay there now, we'll have everybody else following you and somebody will have an accident.'

'Come on, Holly,' said Freddy. 'There's no point in arguing.'

'We won't be able to see a thing behind all those other people,' Holly protested, but she followed him down across the rocks to the back of the beach, where most of their classmates were already standing.

'This is useless,' Holly growled as she jostled for position. 'It's my whale and I can't see a thing.'

What made it worse was that she looked round to see Marjorie Daws, together with Alice Hodson, leaning out of the top window of her mother's shop, which was right opposite the beach. They must have a perfect view from there.

'Leave it to me,' Freddy said.

He began to push his way forward through the crowd, to the annoyance of some, and Holly kept close behind. They reached the barrier, then Freddy yelled loudly to his mother. As soon as she saw him, she signalled to Constable McKee that it was all right to let him through, and he, in turn, gestured to Holly to follow him.

She didn't need to be told twice. She ducked under one of the barriers, then ran down the beach after him. Just at that moment, a great wave rolled in and splashed over the whale's tail. A huge cheer rose up from the watching crowd, and Holly jumped up and down.

'I'm here, Finnegan,' she cried. 'I'm here.'

The whale thrashed its tail briefly, which was greeted by another loud cheer. Holly was delighted that he acknowledged her – well, why shouldn't she think that? She turned in triumph to wave at Marjorie and Alice.

Freddy came to her side. 'Mum reckons he's worse than he was earlier,' he said.

'So would you be if you'd been stuck out in the sun all day when you were supposed to be in the sea,' Holly replied.

'Apparently Piggy Hodson's talking about what they will have to do if he dies.'

'Misery guts,' muttered Holly. 'I bet he wants Finnegan to die just so he can go round being important. Well he's not going to die – as soon as the tide's in he's going to swim away and never come back.'

Another wave flowed over the whale's tail.

'Not long now, Finnegan,' Holly said quietly. She looked back up the beach and saw that her mother had joined the crowd, with George perched precariously on her shoulders. She so wanted her mother to come and stand with her, but she so didn't want George to be there to spoil this magical moment with his pestering.

She waggled her fingers at her mother, who waggled her fingers in reply but didn't move forward.

Holly wandered over to where Big Jim was standing. 'Not long now,' she said.

Big Jim gazed down at her. 'Let's hope he has the strength to get himself away.'

'Can't we help him if not?' Holly asked. 'Can't everyone give him a push when the tide's high enough?'

'He's over twenty metres long and must weigh fifty tons. It's an impossible task. He's on his own in this, I'm afraid, Holly.'

'He'll do it, I know he'll do it,' Holly said firmly.

# Chapter 5

The waves rolled in further and further as the daylight began to fade. Small movements from the whale filled the patient onlookers with hope. The sea rose higher and higher up his side, stroking and caressing him, until at last it engulfed his mouth and eyes and Holly feared he might drown. When the tide reached its peak, everyone held their breath and willed the whale away. Finnegan shuddered and thrashed his tail, but when the tide began to turn, he was still stubbornly resisting its determined pull.

'He doesn't seem to have the strength,' Freddy said quietly.

'Perhaps he's worn out from lying in the sun all day,' said Holly. 'Maybe he'll feel better now it's getting dark and he can rest in peace for a while.'

The islanders were beginning to drift away into the twilight, abandoning their vigil and masking their disappointment with mutterings about late suppers and missed television programmes. Freddy's mother shook her head sadly.

'I really hoped he would do it,' she said.

'It would have been such an amazing sight,' said Freddy.

'He probably didn't want to be watched,' Holly sighed, but even she knew how ridiculous that sounded. She heard her mother calling her to go home, and called back to say that she wouldn't be long. Then she saw the fire engine begin to move away.

'He can't do that!' she cried. 'He can't just leave.'

'Perhaps he's got somewhere else to go,' suggested Freddy.

'What's more important than saving Finnegan?' Holly scoffed.

'Putting a fire out might be,' said Freddy.

'We never have fires on this island,' Holly said adamantly. 'It's much too boring.'

'He's probably gone for something to eat. Finnegan's got plenty of water round him at the moment, and it's not hot any more.'

55

That made Holly feel better. She was worried that Danny Perkins's departure might mean that Finnegan couldn't be saved. She walked over to the group of adults, just to be sure.

'Why's the fire engine gone away?' she demanded.

'He's gone for something to eat and to fill up with water,' said Big Jim.

'Waste of time, though, it is,' huffed Councillor Hodson.

'You don't know that,' Holly countered.

'You've only got to look at the poor beast. There's hardly a breath left in him. Anyway, we can't expect Mr Perkins to stay out here all night.'

Holly glared defiantly at the Councillor, then walked over to the whale. It was true. He did look worse than in the morning. His eyes were closed and, apart from the slightest movement of his ribs, there was nothing else to show that he was alive. Big Jim came up behind her and put his hand on her shoulder.

Holly felt a huge sob swelling in her throat. She pulled away from Big Jim's grasp and tore up the beach. She ran until her legs refused to carry her any further, then she pushed herself on until she reached the rose-cloaked archway into Nana Matty's garden. And there was her grandmother, in the half-light, stooping amongst her beloved chrysanthemums.

'Slugs,' she said disgustedly, as she stood up. 'One of God's lesser creations. And how are you, young lady, apart from out of breath and red as a boiled lobster?'

'Have you seen the whale, Nana?' puffed Holly.

'Yes, I went down to introduce myself this morning,' said Nana Matty, 'and I have a good view of it from my bedroom window.'

'I found him,' said Holly. 'He's called Finnegan and he's a fin whale, which is the biggest next to the blue whale.'

'One of God's great creations,' mused Nana Matty, 'though this one seems to be in a spot of bother.'

'They think he's going to die,' said Holly, then to her annoyance she burst into tears.

Nana Matty put her arms round her and Holly breathed in the comforting smell of lily of the valley. 'Come inside and I'll make you one of Nana's specials.'

Even at the age of eighty and less than five feet tall, Nana Matty was a bundle of energy. Her eyes twinkled mischievously, her elfin face was translucent. Everyone called her Nana Matty, though she was a real grand-mother only to Holly and George. There wasn't a home on this side of the island that didn't boast one of her quilts or jumpers or scarves. On her own since her Geoffrey had passed away from the 'pneumony' twenty years earlier, she spent her days in her armchair knitting and sewing, in her kitchen concocting her 'specials', or in her garden talking to her roses and her 'mums'.

Holly followed her into her cottage and sat down at the tiny kitchen table, while Nana Matty piled cream and quince jam on to a freshly baked scone.

'They're not doing enough to save him, Nana,' Holly sniffed.

'Sometimes nature needs to take its course,' Nana Matty said gently, setting two scones on a plate in front of Holly. 'Your whale might have beached because he's ill and didn't have the strength to resist the tide.'

Holly bit hungrily into a warm scone, cream oozing out from the sides and plopping on to the plate.

'I still think they could do more,' she grumbled. 'Even Danny Perkins has gone away now.'

'They can't do much more except wait for the tide to come back in again and see what happens,' said Nana

Matty, pointing to the white moustache framing Holly's mouth.

Holly wiped the cream away and licked it from her hand. 'We could all help to give it a push when the tide comes in,' she said.

Nana Matty looked at her with a mixture of amusement and sympathy. 'That would be like a nest of ants trying to push a dog,' she smiled. 'Your whale must weigh over fifty tons.'

'That's what Big Jim said, but we could use ropes and tractors,' Holly persisted.

'Nature must deal with it as it will,' Nana Matty said firmly. 'It's very sad, but there's nothing more anyone can do.'


It was dark by the time Holly trekked back up the road towards Lobster Pot Cottage. She took one last lingering look at the blackened shape on the moonlit beach.

'Goodbye, Finnegan,' she whispered. 'The tide will be back again to fetch you in the night. You can steal away while no one is watching.'

She opened the front door of the cottage to be

engulfed by the delicious smells of her mother's blackberry and apple pie, but even that failed to lift her gloom, especially since Nana Matty's scones were still sitting heavily in her stomach. She went to her room to escape George's endless chattering, resisted the temptation to gaze out of her window, and pulled her drawing of Finnegan out of her school bag. She stuck it on her wall and sighed deeply.

'Nobody else seems to care,' she murmured.

# Chapter 6

When Holly woke the next morning it was already light. She snuggled down under Nana Matty's quilt, at the delicious realisation that it was Saturday. She lay there listening to the sounds of her mother clattering plates and her father scolding George, until thoughts of her whale swam into her mind.

'Finnegan!' she squealed. 'Has he gone?'

She leapt out of bed, but hesitated just as she was about to pull back the curtains. She didn't know whether she wanted her whale to be there or not. Her head wanted him to be far, far away; her heart wanted him to be there on the beach, waiting for her. She lead with her head and peered through the curtains, determined to be happy at her whale's departure. What she saw filled her heart with the most enormous joy, but that joy was instantly dispelled. Finnegan was still there, but a small group of islanders was gathered next to him. She was furious that she wasn't there with him as well. She threw on some clothes and stormed downstairs.

'Why didn't you wake me up?' she growled at her startled mother.

'It's Saturday, Holly. You never get up this early on a Saturday.'

'But the whale's still there,' Holly exclaimed.

'It's dead,' announced George.

Holly glared at her brother. 'Don't say that!'

'It's dead, it's dead, it's dead,' chanted George.

'I'm afraid it's true, love,' her mother said gently. 'Your father's been down to the beach already this morning and came back to tell us. They're all down there now, deciding what to do with it.'

Holly felt her stomach churn like a tumble dryer, then, as a great sob rose in her throat, she ran out of the house and away down the winding path. She reached the rocks, climbed to the top and stopped. She didn't know if she wanted to go any closer, and in any case she didn't want the whole village to see that she was crying. She sat down and angrily wiped her eyes.

'They should have done more,' she growled. 'They could have done more.'

She gazed at her whale. He dwarfed all of the onlookers, and his sheer scale somehow made his death even more poignant. Councillor Hodson was there, and, standing importantly by his side, was Alice. He was talking to Holly's father, Big Jim, Danny Perkins and Peter Marshall, who owned the island's only hotel. In another cluster, Freddy was talking with Mr Rowland, Marjorie Daws, Benjamin Westcott and, much to her amazement, Old Ma Meldrew.

'Go back to your cauldron,' Holly hissed into the wind.

Her proclaimed ownership of the whale suddenly spurred her into action. She shinned down the rocks and tore across the beach.

'Why couldn't we have saved him?' she cried. 'We should have been able to save him.'

The islanders turned to gaze at her as she put her arms round her father. 'You should have woken me up,' she scolded, trying to replace her sadness with anger as her eyes pricked with tears again.

'There was nothing anyone could do, Holly,' her father tried to comfort her.

'That whale was ill,' Alice joined in. 'Daddy said that from the beginning.'

'It's a question now of what to do with it,' said Councillor Hodson. 'It'll be a health hazard in no time if we don't get it moved.'

'Shall I fetch a wheelbarrow?' Holly offered.

'It won't fit into –' Alice broke off. Benjamin Westcott sniggered. Then, huffily, Alice continued, 'You think you're so funny, Holly Wainwright.'

'I shall go and ring the council right away and ask them to send someone over,' Councillor Hodson wheezed.

'Hold on a minute there, Reg,' interjected Peter Marshall. 'That whale could be valuable to us as a tourist attraction.'

Holly gazed at him with instant adoration, and gratitude for this support. Peter Marshall was youngish, handsome and single. He had moved to the island three years ago to escape the rat race, and had transformed the hotel from a sour-smelling, paint-popping, paper-peeling old wreck into a smart, comfortable sanctuary for tourists and birdwatchers.

'What on earth are you talking about?' Councillor Hodson snapped. 'Tourist attraction my foot. It's more likely to get us quarantined if the authorities think it could spread disease.'

Old Ma Meldrew suddenly sprang to life. 'We don't need any more of them tourists ploughing up our roads and leaving their litter all over the place.'

'You couldn't be more wrong, Margaret, if I may say so,' argued Peter Marshall. 'It's the money those tourists spend here that helps to give us some sort of independence.'

'Poppycock,' retorted Old Ma Meldrew. 'It might keep you and your fancy hotel going, but it's fishing and farming that pays for everything else.'

'I've got to defend Peter here,' Holly's father jumped in. 'We all benefit from the money tourists spend, especially now that our fishing is restricted. The more tourists the better, I say.'

'Pah!' spat Old Ma Meldrew. 'Your arguments won't wash with me. If I never saw another tourist on this island, I would stand on the top of those rocks and yell Hallelujah. And the sooner that whale's got rid of the better, if you want my opinion.'

'I'd stand on those rocks and wave my knickers in the air if I never saw you on this island again,' mused Holly to herself as the old woman plodded away across the beach.

'Well, I'll be off too then.' Councillor Hodson's rasping tones broke through Holly's thoughts. 'Whatever the council says we should do, we will do, and no more of this nonsense about tourist attractions. A dead whale is a dead whale, and this particular dead whale is a headache I could do without.'

He too set off across the beach, Alice clutching his hand and turning back every so often to see what effect their departure was having on the remaining group.

'That's told us, then,' said Big Jim. 'The arrival on our island of a rare whale, dead or alive, seems to me rather momentous, but as far as Reg is concerned it's a headache.'

'What exactly did you have in mind when you talked about it as a tourist attraction?' Holly's father asked Peter Marshall.

'I don't know exactly. I just thought perhaps we might be able to use its skeleton or part of its skeleton in some way or other.'

Holly winced. She didn't like the thought of Finnegan being reduced to nothing but bones. But she liked the idea that part of him at least might stay on the island.

'What about his teeth?' she said excitedly. 'Perhaps we could keep his teeth.' And then she felt so stupid when she saw the puzzlement on Freddy's face and remembered that Finnegan was a fin whale and that fin whales have a thing called a baleen instead of teeth. 'I mean his tail,' she corrected quickly. 'Or his fins.'

'I'm with all of you on this,' Mr Rowland joined in. 'Nothing has excited the children as much as this whale, and we should keep something of it as a memento for ourselves, not just as a tourist attraction.'

Holly looked fondly at the Head. She had always thought he was an all right person really, and now he had confirmed it for her.

'Well,' said Big Jim, 'let's wait and see what the mainland says, and decide what to do from there.'

# Chapter 7

The tide came and went, lapping round the whale, but the whale was unmoved. The weather became overcast and squally rain blew in. At first the islanders couldn't resist trooping down to the beach to study every inch of the fallen Goliath, touching its velvet-smooth skin and marvelling at its tiny eyes. But their wonder soon turned to boredom, and before the weekend was over, Finnegan lay there all the more forlorn-looking in his abandonment.

Holly had felt his skin and gazed at his tiny eyes and run her hand along his tail fin. She had yelled at any children who had tried to climb on top of him. She wanted to burn a picture of Finnegan into her mind so that she would never forget him. Then, when the weather turned, she peered out at him through the runnels of rain obscuring the view from her bedroom window.

'At least it's not hot now,' she whispered. 'At least you've been left in peace.'

In the middle of the night, she could pretend that he had disappeared back into the ocean as his dark shape blended into the blackness, and she dreamt of swimming with him to faraway lands.

She covered her ears when her mother began to talk about the health hazard her whale would represent if he wasn't dealt with quickly, and she took an angry swipe at George when he hurtled round the kitchen shouting, 'Silly whale, smelly whale, nasty, horrible, stinky whale.' It was bad enough that Finnegan had died. She didn't want to know about what might happen next. Even Freddy had begun to talk about that, and she had shut him up with her most ferocious snarl. As for Alice, Holly kept well clear of her when she heard that the Councillor's daughter had been spreading rumours that Finnegan would have to be dismembered.

School on Monday was agony. Holly arrived to find that Alice was already centre stage in the playground, thrilling her audience with gruesome details of how her father thought Finnegan would have to be cut into small pieces and bagged up like rubbish. Some of the children were clearly upset by what she was saying, others wanted more gory information. Holly hated her for reducing Finnegan to nothing more than a heap of rotting meat.

Her good friend Rosie Atkins joined her and complained that Alice was making her feel sick. They were relieved when the bell went for the start of classes, and even more relieved when Mrs Hardaway forbade any more talk of whales so that they could concentrate on algebra.

It didn't prevent Alice from leaning across and whispering, 'Daddy's talking to the mainland this morning. He thinks they might want the whale's skeleton to go to a museum.'

Holly felt an instant rush of indignation. Why should a museum on the mainland think it could take away her whale just like that? Finnegan hadn't landed on the mainland, had he? He had landed on their island. The mainland hadn't had to watch and worry over him. The mainland hadn't had the trauma of seeing him die. Let them find their own whale, not steal somebody else's. She gave Alice a withering look, then pretended to concentrate on her work. She couldn't concentrate though. She wanted to go and talk to the Head, to her father, to Big Jim, to Peter Marshall. They wouldn't stand for it, would they, not after what they were saying earlier?

At the end of the day she walked back down the road with Freddy and Rosie. When they turned the corner, they were puzzled to see a line of workmen hammering posts into the sand from one end of the beach to the other, several metres behind the whale.

'What are they doing that for?' Holly asked.

'Beats me,' said Freddy.

They hurried down the road, ducking below the windowsill of Lobster Pot Cottage, and headed towards the rocks. As they scrambled over the other side, one of the workmen called out, 'Hey, the beach is out of bounds. You'll have to go back.'

They couldn't believe what they were hearing.

'What do you mean the beach is out of bounds?' Freddy called back.

'Health and safety,' said the workman. 'You can't come on it until this whale has been disposed of.'

'What, in case it bites?' cried Holly.

'There's no need to be cheeky, young lady. I'm just doing my job.'

Just then, Holly caught sight of Constable McKee striding towards them.

'I'm sorry, but the beach is closed until further notice,' the Constable informed them.

'What if we want to go for a swim?' Holly asked.

'Well, you will have to go to the next cove instead.'

'What about if we want to build sandcastles?' joined in Rosie.

'The sand on the next beach is just as good,' Constable McKee humoured them. 'Now get on with you before I lose my patience.'

'What's going to happen?' asked Holly.

'We don't know yet, Holly. Someone from the mainland is coming across tomorrow and we'll decide then.'

'Someone from the mainland,' mimicked Holly as they clambered back over the rocks. 'Dad gets really cross that we always have to ask the mainland what to do.'

'We should declare independence,' cried Freddy, coming to a halt, standing bolt upright and punching his fist in the air. 'This island is now FREE!' he yelled. 'Long live our island. Hip hip –'

'Hooray!' yelled Holly and Rosie.

They raced up the winding path. Just before they separated at the top, Holly said fiercely, 'We're gonna keep our whale, aren't we?'

'Too right,' said Freddy.

'You bet,' said Rosie.

# Chapter 8

Holly, Freddy and Rosie hurried out of school the next day, but not before Alice had told them that the whale would soon stink the island out according to her father, and that the maggots would have a field day.

'Poor Finnegan,' said Holly to her friends as they reached the bend in the road. 'If only the sea hadn't left him behind in the first place.'

'Can't they just get a digger or something and roll him back into the sea?' Rosie asked.

Freddy looked at her quizzically. 'They would need a crane to lift him, and anyway they wouldn't be able to take him out far enough.'

'The sea's where he belongs, though,' said Holly

wistfully. 'I wish a huge wave would carry him away.'

'It had better not be now,' grinned Freddy. 'Your father's on the beach.'

They were close enough to the beach to pick out Councillor Hodson and Constable McKee talking with two men they didn't recognise. Standing near them, Holly's father, Peter Marshall, Big Jim and Danny Perkins were listening to what was being said. By the time the three children had reached the road along the back of the beach, the group with Holly's father had joined Councillor Hodson, Constable McKee and the strangers, and voices were being raised.

'Sounds like they're arguing,' said Freddy.

'Go for it, Dad,' Holly urged. 'Tell them what's what.'

They were about to jump on to the sand to approach the adults, when Holly's father saw them and waved them away.

'Not now, Holly,' he said sharply, then turned back to the group.

Holly, Freddy and Rosie stopped in their tracks. The

adults lowered their voices, but it was clear from the waving arms that the discussion was heated. The three friends hovered for a moment, before Freddy took a step to walk sideways across the beach.

'What are you doing, Freddy?' Holly hissed. 'Why shouldn't we join in, just because we're children? It's as much our concern as theirs.'

'Grown-ups always think children are in the way,' said Rosie. 'It's as if what we think doesn't matter.'

'There's no point in arguing now,' Freddy said firmly. 'Let's wait and see what's been decided, then we can have our say.'

'I want those men from the mainland to know what we think,' Holly insisted. 'It might make them change their minds.'

'We don't even know what they think yet,' Freddy argued. 'They might be on our side for all we know.'

'Doubt it,' said Holly. 'Not by the look of things.'

Just at that moment, Holly's father turned and walked away from the group. Big Jim followed with the fireman, while Peter Marshall continued to argue. Holly ran up to her father and grabbed his arm.

'What's happening, Dad? What are they going to do with Finnegan?'

'It seems that a museum on the mainland wants his skeleton. They haven't got a fin whale in their collection.'

'We haven't even got a collection,' Holly spluttered. 'We haven't got anything on our poxy island. No wonder nobody wants to come here, and everybody here wants to leave. Even the sheep are bored.'

Her father grinned. 'Been speaking to them recently, have you?'

'Baaaaa,' she said sourly. 'Anyway, what's to stop us keeping the skeleton for ourselves if we want to?'

'Holly, believe me, I'm with you on this, and I'm not the only one. But various procedures have to be gone through first before we can start laying claim to any part of the whale, and we need the council's help to dispose of its flesh. Nobody here has the equipment or know-how.'

Holly flinched. 'Don't talk about that. I don't want to talk about that.'

'It's life, Holly,' her father said gently. 'Life's not always pretty.'

'It's death,' Holly murmured, 'and I don't like it.'

Her father put his arm through hers. She rested her head against his shoulder as they walked up the road to Lobster Pot Cottage.

'I bet the mainland gets its way,' she said just before they went through the front door.

'We'll see,' said her father.

I hate 'we'll see', thought Holly. 'We'll see' is one of those expressions grown-ups use to fob children off when they already know the answer and don't want to admit it. Well, I refuse to be fobbed off.

'They'll have to fight us,' she said and waited for his reaction.

Her father looked at her, then grinned and ruffled her hair.

'I think you might be right,' he nodded.

Trog launched himself at them when they went into the kitchen, followed by George who was making aeroplane noises.

'Guess what, Daddy, Daddy, Daddy,' he shrieked.

'What, what, what?' said his father.

'Troggy did a pooh on the carpet,' said George triumphantly.

'He didn't!' exclaimed Holly's father, looking quizzically at her mother, who came out of the kitchen wiping flour from her hands.

'Did, did, did,' squealed George. 'A great big smelly poohy stinky one, and Mummy had to clear it up with a bucket of hot bubbly water and it made her feel sick.'

Trog whined, scratched his ear and licked Holly's hand, as her mother grimaced and said, 'I can't understand it. I'd only popped out into the backyard to hang up some washing. He didn't even scratch at the door until it was too late.'

'We'll have to teach him how to cross his legs,' said Holly. 'Poor old Trog.'

'Poor old Mum, more like,' said her father. 'Well, it might be after the horse has bolted, but I'll take him out for a walk.'

'I'm coming too, I'm coming too,' shrieked George. 'I want to see the horse that's bolted.'

Holly smirked at her mother, glad that they were going to be on their own for a little while. She watched as her father and brother encouraged Trog down the winding path, then grabbed a handful of biscuits from the tin and sat down at the kitchen table.

'Why do we always have to do what the mainland says, Mum?' she asked.

'Because we're too small and don't have the resources to look after ourselves, love,' her mother replied. 'They own us, effectively, like a large company might own a small company, and we rely on them for many of our day-to-day needs.'

'Doesn't mean they have to take everything from us and tell us what to do all the time,' said Holly.

'It's just the way it is. We're answerable to them over most things, but I think you'll find that if we feel strongly enough about something we can put up a good fight.'

'I feel strongly enough about Finnegan. So do lots of the children in my school, and Dad does and Big Jim and Peter Marshall,' Holly said, 'but most people don't seem to care.'

'So what are you going to do about it?' her mother challenged her.

'Me?' Holly said incredulously. 'What can I do?'

'You can use that determination and stubbornness of

yours, for a start, and you can galvanise your friends into action.'

'What does galvanise mean?'

'It means to spark someone or something into action. For instance, you could begin a petition, or a poster campaign.' Her mother grinned. 'You could lobby old Hodson.'

'Huh! He won't listen,' Holly scoffed. 'He thinks the whale's a nuisance.'

'He'll have to listen if enough people have a go at him.'

'Dad says we should wait and see what happens,' said Holly.

'That doesn't stop you drawing up battle plans in case,' said her mother. 'At least it will make you feel as if you're doing something.'

Holly liked the idea of drawing up battle plans. It made her feel as if she could make things happen instead of sitting around waiting for them to happen to her.

'Yeah, you're right, Mum,' she said. 'We can be ready and waiting for them. They won't know what's hit them.'

She ran upstairs to her bedroom. While the house was still quiet, she could concentrate on creating her first moves.

SAVE OUR WHALE, she wrote in large letters across a sheet of paper. Just the act of putting down those three words filled her with optimism. KEEP FINNEGAN HERE, she wrote on another sheet of paper. TELL THE MAINLAND 'HANDS OFF', DON'T LET THE MAINLAND HAVE OUR WHALE, FINNEGAN IS OUR WHALE. We could put posters up all over the island, Holly thought gleefully. Freddy would help, and Rosie, and lots of the others. It could be a project in school. She was sure Mr Rowland would let them. Dad could drive them round the island to stick the posters up.

She dug out from her desk the picture she had drawn of a fin whale and wondered how she could use it as part of the poster. And then she had a brainwave. Nana Matty was artistic. Nana Matty did the posters for the Christmas ceilidh. Together they could do the most amazing posters. Everyone would stop and look at them, and everyone would want to be on their side – well, nearly everyone. Everyone except Councillor Hodson and Old Ma Meldrew, and a few other miserable old fossils. Who wanted them on their side anyway?

Holly couldn't wait for the next day so that she could talk to her schoolfriends about her plans. And then she would tell Nana Matty. As soon as the mainland tried to take their whale, they would spring into action.

# Chapter 9

Holly bounced out of bed the next morning, scribbled down two more ideas for posters that had prised their way through her dreams, and tore back the curtains. Rain was spilling down the windows from the leaky gutter above, blurring the outlook and playing tricks with her eyes. She couldn't tell whether or not there were people on the beach, and it looked as if parts of her whale were dissolving, trickling away, then flowing back together again. Like a mirage, Holly thought, except it doesn't rain in the desert.

She scrambled downstairs to a breakfast of eggs on toast. Trog was sizzling by the range, and didn't bat an eyelid when she clattered into the kitchen.

'A good morning to you too,' she aimed at him. 'Cat got your tongue?'

'Troggy's a tired, soggy doggy,' said George. 'Big Jim took him for a walk.'

'Poor Trog,' said her mother. 'He's getting too old to keep up with Jim's collies, but I was delighted not to have to go out myself.'

'Is Dad fishing?' Holly asked.

'Round the other side of the island,' her mother replied. 'He won't be back till late this evening.'

'What do you think will happen today?' Holly asked.

'I hope they'll catch a lot of fish,' smiled her mother.

'Oh, Mum,' cried Holly, 'you know I didn't mean that.'

'Oooohhhh, Mum,' repeated George.

'Your guess is as good as mine, and my guess is not very much. Apart from anything else, the weather is atrocious, and secondly it'll take a while before anything happens if I know how these sorts of things work.'

'But this isn't like any other sort of thing,' protested Holly. 'This is a unique sort of thing.'

'That makes it worse,' said her mother. 'It just means that everyone will be faffing around not knowing what to do, and passing the buck to everyone else. To be fair, though, it's a very big job we're talking about here.'

'Well, I'm ready,' pouted Holly, 'so I don't see why they can't be.'

'That's because *you're* a unique sort of thing,' her mother grinned. 'Woe betide those mainlanders if they do have to deal with you. They won't know what's hit them.'

'Will you help?'

'You just try and stop me. I'll have my frying pan at the ready.'

'Sausages! Cook sausages!' shrieked George.

'Never mind sausages,' laughed Holly's mother. 'Let's get you two off to school. Peggy's picking you up in a minute.'

Holly didn't mind being given a lift by Peggy Daws when it rained, but it meant sitting in the back of her car with her annoying seven-year-old daughter, Bella, as well as George, while Marjorie sprawled gloating in the front. Peggy was a plump, jovial woman with an infectious laugh. She ran the village shop and post office, where she was the fountain of all gossip and where her love of chocolate frequently meant that it was in short supply on the shelves.

Sitting in the back of the car today, with Bella sucking loudly on a lollipop and Marjorie going on about her invite to Alice's birthday party, Holly was bursting to talk about her campaign, but Marjorie was one of the last people she wanted to support her. Not only that, but it was too soon for the fountain of all gossip to hear about it, though she might be useful later on, and Holly certainly didn't want Bella and George to think they could be part of it. Instead, she focused on the windscreen wipers, which were struggling to keep the windscreen clear, and tried to block out the slurping next to her ear.

'It's a mucky old day today and no mistake,' Peggy chortled. 'If this rain goes on much longer, that whale will think its made its way back to the sea.'

'That whale can't think, Mum,' said Marjorie.

'That whale's dead,' piped up George.

'Clever,' said Marjorie. 'Alice says they might have to blow it up to get rid of it.'

Holly was about to explode herself, when Peggy said, 'Don't talk nonsense, dear. They couldn't possibly be thinking of blowing it up. We'd have blubber everywhere.'

'Boom!' yelled George.

'Yuck,' slurped Bella.

'Well, that's what Alice says,' retorted Marjorie, 'and she should know because her dad's dealing with it.'

'Well, I'll certainly have something to say about it if that's the case,' said Peggy. 'My shop's right opposite the beach.'

To Holly's intense relief, they had reached the school gates. She thanked Peggy, then dashed across the playground and into school, before Marjorie could attempt to walk in with her. There were still five minutes left until lessons started – time for Holly to pull Freddy aside and tell him what Marjorie had said.

'They wouldn't do that, would they?' she asked anxiously.

'Only if they're really stupid,' Freddy grinned. 'I was looking on the internet about how to deal with a dead whale, and I read that they tried that once in Oregon. The explosion sent these massive pieces of blubber flying all over the place, including all over the crowd who were watching.'

'Serves them right,' chuckled Holly, then she told him about her idea for posters and a petition, and how she was going to get the whole island to protest if the mainland tried to take their whale away.

'You'll help, won't you, Freddy? Mum said she would as well, and I'm going to ask Nana Matty to help make the posters.'

'My mum and dad will sign a petition. They hate the way the mainland interferes in our business.'

'Do you think she'll help?' Holly whispered, pointing in Mrs Hardaway's direction as she entered the class-room.

'She might,' Freddy whispered back.

The rain was still pouring down at lunchtime, much to Holly's dismay. It meant that they had to stay in the classroom after they had finished eating in the dining hall. She wouldn't be able to discuss her plans with her close friends without everyone else trying to listen in. It wasn't long, though, before the subject of the whale was raised. Marjorie asked Mrs Hardaway if she thought the whale should be blown up, which resulted in half the class whooping with delight and making bomb noises. Holly stuck her fingers in her ears while Mrs Hardaway tried to calm things down, then listened with delight when her teacher said that blowing up the whale was 'the most ridiculous notion'. Alice became indignant and argued that her father, who should know, had said it was a possibility.

'If they do that, then the mainland won't have a skeleton to put into its museum,' Holly said triumphantly.

Alice looked rather uncertain for a moment, but continued, 'Perhaps it won't hurt the skeleton as long as they don't use too much dynamite.'

'Oh, yeah, like they can be so accurate,' scoffed Freddy.

'I think blowing it up is a little unlikely, Alice,' said Mrs Hardaway, trying to mollify her, 'but, of course, I'm no expert.'

The discussion continued for a while longer, everyone with their own idea of how the whale should be dealt with, until Mrs Hardaway called them all to order because it was time to resume lessons. Holly breathed a sigh of relief and longed for the end of the day.

★  ★  ★

When it came at last, the rain had stopped, so at least Holly didn't have to put up with Marjorie on the way home. She set off down the road with Freddy and Rosie, and was happy to elaborate on her plans for a poster campaign and petition. Rosie became very excited.

'My aunt and uncle live on the other side of the island and they'll help,' she said, 'and my mum and dad will sign, I know they will, and my brothers.'

Rosie Atkins was the sort of person you wanted to have on your side, Holly thought. She was a bit of a boffin, but good fun. She lived with her parents and twin brothers in a tiny cottage on the road beyond the beach. Her father fished with Holly's father, and her mother was a receptionist at the hotel. Her brothers, who were seven years older than her, collected and read the news at the island's radio station as DJ Dum and DJ Dee. They were hoping to be discovered one day and whisked off to the mainland to begin careers as disc jockeys on national radio.

Holly found herself wanting the mainland to insist upon taking her whale. She was itching to start creating posters and collecting names on a petition. It would be the most exciting thing she had ever done, and, when they won, when the council gave in, everybody on the island would cheer her. Right now, though, she could see that something was happening on the beach. Two men were by the whale's head, watched by a scattering of islanders from behind the rope barrier. One of the men was delving into a large bag, the other took something from him and knelt down by the whale.

'What are they doing?' Holly demanded. 'Come on, let's go and see.'

They ran down the road as quickly as they could. When they reached the rope barrier, they asked Peter Marshall, who was one of the onlookers, what was happening.

'Two vets from the mainland,' he explained, 'taking samples to find out why the whale died.'

'Couldn't my mum have done that?' said Freddy indignantly.

'I suppose they needed experts,' said Peter Marshall doubtfully, 'though they might at least have involved her.'

'Too right,' said Holly. 'It would make a change from sheep.'

Freddy stared at her crossly. 'She doesn't just look after sheep. She's had to deal with all sorts of injured animals and birds, even seals.'

'Now that the authorities on the mainland are involved,' the hotel owner continued, 'they'll want to use all their own people. That's just the way it is.'

'So we're just supposed to stand by and watch,' Freddy complained, 'even though the whale landed on our island.'

'Apparently, according to an ancient law, any whale longer than twenty-five feet that beaches on the mainland, or on any of its islands, belongs to the Crown.'

'The Crown? What does that mean?'

'Her Majesty the Queen.'

Holly was stunned. 'What would the Queen want with a whale?' she spluttered.

'It would be a great talking point in front of the palace,' Freddy said sourly.

'Whales don't belong in the middle of a city,' said Holly. 'Dead or alive, they should be near the sea.'

'I think, in our case, that the Crown will leave its representatives to decide what should happen, and my guess is that it will definitely wind up in a heritage museum,' Peter suggested.

'Surrounded by a load of old fossils,' muttered Freddy.

Holly was desperate to ask Peter whether he would join with them in mounting a protest if the worst came to the worst, but she bit her tongue. It was still too early to let other people in on their plans. Besides, knowing grown-ups they would try to take it over. Instead, she asked when he thought they might come to a decision.

'Who knows?' Peter said. 'It could be days, weeks or even months. The wheels of bureaucracy can move very fast or very slowly. More often than not, it's very slowly.'

'But they can't leave the whale here to stink the place out,' said Freddy.

'No, they'll have to deal with the flesh as a matter of urgency, but they can take all the time they like with the skeleton. After all, nobody's going to walk off with it.'

# Chapter 10

It was several more days before anything else happened. By then, the islanders were beginning to complain about the increasingly unpleasant smell carried to them across the beach by the wind. Some of them complained about the beach being out of bounds, which meant that they had to take the long way round to the ferry, so that it was further to walk to and from it. Some people complained too about the number of mainlanders catching the ferry across to the island just to see the whale.

'We don't want them busybodies trekking backwards and forwards, gawping at us like we're some sort of weird species,' grumbled Old Ma Meldrew to Holly's mother over the garden gate.

Holly gawped and sniggered.

'I'm sure you're imagining that,' smiled Holly's mother.

'Don't even bother to say hello, most of them,' Old Ma Meldrew rasped. 'They just swan past as if they own the place. Ignorant they are.'

'Well, Peggy's happy. It's doubled her takings in the shop.'

'Peggy's a fool for encouraging them.'

Cyril Blackburn, the postman, complained that it was taking him a lot longer to do his round, because everyone wanted to know what was happening all the time, especially those famillies who lived too far away from the beach to see what was happening for themselves. And then people were complaining that their post was arriving late.

'It's hardly my fault if everyone keeps asking me what's going on,' he moaned to Holly's father one morning. 'Half the time people who are complaining about their post being late are making me even later because of their complaining, and because they themselves are asking what's happening.'

'It must be difficult being the one person everyone

turns to for the latest news,' Holly's father said sympathetically.

'Well, of course, I don't mind really,' the postman replied. 'I like to keep myself abreast of things, but it's all getting a bit out of hand.'

'Well, Cyril, you'd better be off or you'll be late again,' said her father, waving his hand in front of his face as he closed the door.

'Somebody should tell him,' Holly grimaced. 'He's more of a health hazard than our whale.'

Councillor Hodson complained that everyone was blaming him for the delay in dealing with the whale.

'I can't be held responsible if the mainland are dragging their feet,' he huffed. 'Besides, disposing of the whale is a job that requires experts, and experts aren't to be found at the drop of a hat.'

'They'd be here fast enough if there was a risk the whale might escape,' observed Big Jim.

At school, Alice said that it wasn't fair that everyone was blaming her father. 'Daddy says he's done all he can, and Mummy says he has more important things than a dead animal to deal with, and people should realise that.'

She put her fingers in her ears when Freddy said that

the whale was the most important thing because it was attracting vermin and the stench was making people feel ill.

'It's not her dad's fault,' Marjorie Daws piped up. 'He can't make people come if they don't want to.'

But Holly's father said it showed just how ineffective the Councillor was, and that if he was in the Councillor's position he would create such a stink that the local authority would have to send people over to sort things out.

'And how would you do that?' Holly's mother asked. 'I'm sure Reg is doing his best.'

Holly glared at her mother. Why did she always have to be so − nice?

'I'd start by threatening to write to the national newspapers and saying that the health of a small island community is being put at risk because of the mainland's failure to take action,' her father said firmly.

'Why can't we do that anyway?' demanded Holly. 'Why do we have to wait for Piggy Hodson?'

'Don't call him that, please,' said her mother.

'Dad does,' Holly pouted. 'Anyway, why can't we tell the papers?'

'Because it would be going behind Pi— Councillor Hodson's back. And I'm sure things will start to happen in the next day or so,' her mother said.

Things did start to happen, the very next day. Holly was snatched from her sleep by a hullabaloo from the garden. She leapt from her bed and threw open the bedroom window on to a misty morning. Below, the hens were squawking blue murder, while Trog was howling his head off. A shadowy figure was scurrying away down the winding path, hampered, it seemed, by a large object in its mouth.

The back door opened and Holly's father yelled, 'That poxy fox!' before taking off down the path after it. Trog tried to follow but the garden gate slammed in his face. He howled even more loudly, continuing his role as protector of the chickens, which were still squawking blue murder. Holly's mother appeared at the door to see what the fuss was about.

'I think the fox has stolen one of our chickens,' Holly called down.

'Not again!' cried her mother.

'Poxy fox, poxy fox,' shrieked George, who arrived

suddenly and wound himself round Trog's neck. 'You should have stopped him, Troggy,' he scolded, while Trog tried to escape to the sanctuary of the kitchen.

'How on earth did he get in this time?' Holly's mother exclaimed.

'He's dug another hole under the dratted fence.' Her father's voice came out of the gloom.

'Did he drop the hen?' Holly asked.

' 'Fraid not, love.'

Her father came back through the gate, still in his dressing gown and slippers, and padded over to the henhouse.

'The latch couldn't have been down properly,' he said.

Holly felt a large pang of guilt. She had been the one to lock up the previous evening. She hoped to goodness that the rest of the hens were all right, and wondered which one the fox had taken.

'It's my turn to get the eggs,' George shouted, and ran after his father in his pyjamas.

'No, George, not now,' his mother called out. 'Let Dad calm the hens down first.'

Holly could see from her window that there was a

hen lying by the fence. She gulped and bit her lip. It was her favourite, Mrs Frillyknickers. She had named her herself, and always had a fit of the giggles when she watched her skedaddle across the yard, bottom waggling, Cosmo the cock in hot pursuit. It looked as if her skedaddling days were over, poor Mrs Frillyknickers.

George had spotted her now and was heading towards her with a stick.

'Leave her, George!' Holly yelled out of the window.

She hurtled downstairs and out through the back door, past her startled mother. She grabbed George by the elbow and pulled him away from the hen's body, just as he was about to prod her.

'Mum, take him indoors,' she cried.

George squirmed angrily in her grasp. 'Leave me alone,' he squealed.

Holly marched him back to her mother, who had realised now what was happening and took him indoors. Her father was just backing out of the henhouse.

'Are they all right, Dad?' she asked anxiously.

'Two missing, the rest in shock.'

'Mrs Frillyknickers is by the fence.' Holly gulped again. 'It looks like her neck's broken.'

'And Mrs Moneypenny is about to be the fox's breakfast,' her father sighed, heading over to the fence to pick up Mrs Frillynickers's broken body. 'I suppose we can't blame the fox for doing what comes naturally to him.'

'You can blame me for not locking up properly,' said Holly.

'And I can blame myself for not checking the fence,' her father replied. He put his arm round Holly's shoulder. 'So the fox has made mugs of both of us.'

'I'll miss Mrs Frillyknickers – she was my favourite.'

'Then you can come with me and help me choose her replacement,' her father smiled, squeezing her shoulder tight.

Holly's breakfast egg didn't taste quite the same that morning. It was one of Mrs Frillyknickers's, she knew that by the colour, and she knew too that it was probably the last, unless there was one waiting to be collected. If there were one waiting to be collected, she wondered if her father would let her hatch it out. She grinned at the thought of a Little Miss Frilly-knickers.

As soon as she had finished her breakfast, she nipped out into the garden to check the henhouse before George got there, but Mrs Frillyknickers's favourite nesting box was empty. There would be no Little Miss.

When she came out again, she saw Old Ma Meldrew about to go past the gate. Before she could hide, the old woman had stopped and was looking at the hole under the fence and the scattered feathers.

'Fox been in, I see,' she said. 'Got the lot, did he?'

'Two,' replied Holly reluctantly.

'You were lucky then.'

'We're not lucky if we lost two. We'd only be lucky if we didn't lose any.'

'You're asking for trouble keeping chickens. They're a magnet for vermin, just like that heap of rotting flesh on the beach down there.'

'You mouldy old misery,' Holly muttered under her breath, as their neighbour made her way back to her cottage.

She went back indoors to get ready for school.

'You won't just put Mrs Frillyknickers out with the rubbish, will you?' she asked her parents.

'What would you like us to do with her?' her father asked.

Holly thought for a moment. 'Can we bury her under the apple tree? It has frilly blossom in the spring so it will remind me of her.'

# Chapter 11

Alice came into the school playground that day and announced that work was about to begin on the whale. A team of experts with specialist equipment was heading for the island, and it might be days before they would finish.

'Daddy says everyone on the mainland is very excited about our find, and lots of whale biologists are coming to study it as they cut it up,' she said. 'Daddy says a man from the ministry is coming as well to discuss what's going to happen with the skeleton, and he's going to stay with us in our house.'

'What, the skeleton?' Holly asked, though she knew exactly what Alice meant.

'No, stupid,' Alice retorted. 'The man from the ministry.'

'What's going to happen to all the meaty bits?' asked Marjorie.

'They're going to put them in a pie,' said Freddy.

'If you're not going to be serious, Freddy Roberts, then I shan't tell you any more,' Alice snapped.

'What about all the horrible, yucky, squidgy inside bits?' whooped Alfie Perkins. 'My dad says he wouldn't want to go near the whale's guts 'cos they'll stink and they'll be all full of gas and will explode all over him.'

'We really wanted to know that,' scowled Holly.

'He won't be allowed to go near the whale at all,' said Alice. 'There'll be lots of screens in front of it so that nobody can see, and nobody will be allowed to go on the beach. Except my dad will have to make sure things are going all right and that the experts have got everything they need.'

'Who'd want to watch it anyway?' Rosie joined in. 'It'll be gruesome. I'd rather remember Finnegan the way he was when he was alive.'

'Me too,' said Holly. 'Everyone's talking about him now as if he was never a living thing. It's like he's become nothing but a big pile of rubbish that needs to be got rid of. Well, I'm not going to listen to any more of your horrible talk because it makes me feel sick, not just in my stomach but in my head.'

She put her arm through Rosie's and steered her away across the playground. Freddy caught up with them as they headed into the school building.

'Do you know they haven't even asked my mum if she wants to help?' he growled. 'Dad's furious.'

'They can't stop her, can they?' said Holly. 'She's the one who works here.'

'Probably not, but she thinks they should at least have spoken to her. I've got a good mind to go and tell Piggy Hodson what I think of him.'

'He's too busy being important to take any notice,' said Holly.

'You wait till we start our petition. He'll soon find out what we think of him then,' grinned Rosie.


On the way home that afternoon, they saw Curly and Betty Lockett driving their taxis up to the island's hotel. Three men climbed out of one taxi, and two men and a woman got out of the other.

Freddy waved at Betty to stop as she drove off.

'Were they the experts?' he asked.

Betty nodded. 'They seem like a friendly enough bunch,' she said. 'They're starting work tomorrow, as soon as the bulldozer, containers and the salvage team arrive. They're going down for a preliminary look at our friend once they've unpacked. They're all fired up about what they might find inside him.'

'Is the Minister here as well?' asked Holly.

'He was called away on urgent business and won't be here for two or three days.'

'That's a bit of a let-down for Piggy,' muttered Freddy. 'I expect he's been up all night with the excitement of the Minister arriving.'

'I expect he made the bed up himself,' chuckled Rosie, and Holly hooted at her friend's quiet sarcasm.

They continued down the road in silence, until they reached the corner where the beach opened up gloomily before them. Finnegan was now cut off from the rest of the world by a stretch of tarpaulins that prevented anyone from seeing him, unless they were on the road to the school, or on top of the rocks. But it was too far away to see very much from the road, and the rocks had been made out of bounds by a rope that was tied all the way round the back of them and signs saying Keep Out.

Piled up within the rope barrier that still ran from one end of the beach to the other were a number of large metal containers.

'Is that where they're going to put him?' asked Rosie.

'Mum says they'll probably put all the blubber and stuff in the containers and take it to landfill sites on the mainland,' said Freddy.

'As long as they leave us Finnegan's skeleton,' said Holly.

'Where would we put the skeleton?' asked Rosie. 'It can't really stay where it is.'

The three friends looked at each other because none of them had really thought about it before.

'It could go at the back of the beach,' said Freddy.

'What about in the school playground?' joked Rosie.

'I bet Peter Marshall would like it in the hotel garden,' said Freddy.

'I bet Piggy Hodson would like it in his back garden,' grinned Holly.

'Alice could use it as a climbing frame,' said Freddy.

They all chortled loudly, until Holly suddenly felt guilty that they were laughing at Finnegan's fate.

'Perhaps it could go by the landing stage so that when visitors come they'll see it straightaway,' she suggested seriously.

'That's a great idea,' said Freddy. 'We could even get Big Jim to rename the ferry after Finnegan.'

They had reached the back of the beach now, just in time to see Big Jim coming out of Peggy Daws's shop. He crossed the road to speak to them.

'Looks like it's all go at last,' he said. 'The experts have arrived and tomorrow I'm to bring over a bulldozer for the salvage team to load those containers.'

'They're enormous,' said Rosie.

'So's our whale,' he smiled.

'We were talking,' said Holly, 'and we thought a good place to put the skeleton would be by the ferry landing stage. And we thought you could name the ferry after him. What do you think?'

Big Jim looked at them quizzically. 'Who says we're going to be allowed to keep the skeleton? From what I've just heard from Peggy, who heard it from Winnie Hodson, the authorities on the mainland are adamant that it is up to them what happens to it and that it's going to be housed in the heritage museum on the mainland. They haven't got a fin whale and they're determined to have this one.'

'And we're just going to let them?' demanded Holly.

Big Jim grinned at her. 'No, Holly,' he said. 'I don't think we are.'

'So we're going to fight?' said Freddy.

'Too right we are,' said Big Jim. 'As soon as the word gets round, which it will very quickly knowing Peggy and Cyril, I think a meeting in the village hall will be called rather urgently.'

'We were planning to have a petition,' said Holly.

'We could collect loads of names at school,' said Rosie.

'Dad can ask all his fishing friends from the other side of the island,' Holly said, becoming more excited by the minute.

'Mum can ask everyone who comes to her surgery and all the farmers she visits,' said Freddy.

'And we thought about posters as well,' Holly added. 'We could even get Postie to stick them on the side of his van.'

'I can see you've got it all arranged then,' laughed Big Jim. 'We adults can just sit back and let you do all the work.'

'We'll need you to help as well,' Holly said seriously. 'The mainland won't listen to a bunch of school-children.'

'Well, that's good then,' Big Jim said, 'because I've got one or two ideas of my own.'

'I'm going to go and see Nana Matty and ask her to do some posters.'

Holly skipped off in the direction of her grand-mother's cottage. She couldn't wait now to start her campaign. If the mainland thought they could have their way over her whale, they were mistaken. She was going to be David to their Goliath. In her head she began to recite the names of the people she knew would sign her petition, and in her head it seemed as though there were thousands, even if the island did have only a hundred and fifty-six inhabitants, and some of those were babies. If more than half of the inhabitants voted to keep Finnegan, it would be enough, wouldn't it?

She knocked on Nana Matty's door.

There was no reply.

'Come on, Nana,' she hissed impatiently. 'This is no time to be having one of your snoozes.'

She tapped on a window and peered through the glass. Apart from her own reflection, nothing moved. Why did Nana Matty have to choose now to be out? She hardly ever went out, except to post letters. Except to pop to the village shop when she ran out of something important and Peggy's girls weren't there to deliver it for her. Except when Miss Marigold came to call in Daisy, her rust-encrusted 'phutmobile', and they chugged off round the island on a 'girls' adventure'.

Except when she came to tea or to babysit. Was that where she was now, at Lobster Pot Cottage, tucking into her daughter's homemade scones, which weren't as good as her own but it was nice to be treated by someone else?

Holly raced back along the road, tripping over her own feet in her anxiety to speak to Nana Matty before her mother whisked her home again. She swung through the front door and into the kitchen, to find her grandmother sitting at the table playing snap with George.

'SNAP!' yelled George, grabbing the pile of cards, as soon as Nana Matty looked up to greet her.

'Ah, there you are, dear,' she smiled. 'Have you been out putting the world in its place?'

'They're not going to let us keep Finnegan's skeleton,' Holly blurted out.

'But we want to keep the skeleton,' protested George.

Holly ignored him. 'Where's Mum?' she asked.

'I'm afraid your mother has had to take Trog to the vet. He seems a little off colour,' said Nana Matty. 'She should be back soon.'

'He was sick all over the comfy chair!' George squealed, leaping back on to his feet. 'Mummy had to scrub and scrub and scrub to clean it off and the chair's all wet now. Daddy won't be able to sit on it tonight and he'll be cross.'

'It's not Trog's fault if he's not well,' Holly bristled.

'Why don't I get you your tea while you tell me about the skeleton,' Nana Matty said quickly.

'Peggy Daws says Mrs Hodson says we're not going to be allowed to keep it on the island,' Holly explained. 'They're saying it's up to the mainland what happens to it and that it's going to be sent away to the heritage museum, which isn't fair because he's our whale.'

'I see,' said Nana Matty, while she cut a large hunk of fruitcake and placed it in front of Holly.

'We're not going to let them take it, Nana,' Holly said determinedly. 'I'm going to start a petition and we're going to do some posters and I thought you could help with them because you're so good at drawing and painting and we need to act quickly before it's too late and Big Jim's got some ideas of his own as well.'

'Play snap, Nana,' George jumped in. 'Play snap now.'

'Just a minute, George,' Nana Matty said firmly, and George instantly quietened down. 'Are you sure enough people will feel the same way as you do about keeping the skeleton?' she asked Holly. 'After all, it will take up a lot of space and not everyone will like the idea of a heap of bones cluttering up the bay.'

'They won't be cluttering up the bay, Nana,' protested Holly. 'It'll be like having a huge sculpture to look at, and lots of people will come over from the mainland just to see it. This island needs more tourists to help the economy. Peter Marshall said so.'

'Some islanders I know hate the very sight of tourists,' Nana Matty smiled.

'I don't know why,' said Holly hotly. 'It makes a change to see some different faces around.'

'I agree with you, dear, and I agree with you that we should keep our skeleton. I'm just preparing you for the fact that not everyone will be behind you. Now, what is it you want me to do?'

'Oh Nana, if you could design some big posters for us saying SAVE OUR WHALE so that we can stick them up by the ferry landing stage and on Postie's van and in Peggy's shop and in the hotel and in the cafe and in the pub and in the village hall and –' Holly gave her grandmother a big hug.

'Well, I am very busy, and it's not long till I need to get out my brushes for the ceilidh, but –'

Just at that moment, they heard the front door open.

'Mummy's back,' George yelled. 'Me go and see Troggy, me go and see Troggy.'

He bounded out into the hall. 'Where's Troggy, Mummy?' they heard him ask.

'Trog's still with the vet, sausage,' Holly's mother replied. 'He's going to sleep there tonight so that Mrs

Roberts can keep an eye on him.'

'Why does she want to keep an eye on him? Is she going to sleep with him? Is she going to let us have him back again tomorrow? She can't keep him for ever, can she? He's our dog.'

'No, she can't keep him for ever, love. We can go and fetch him tomorrow.'

Holly's mother came into the kitchen. She looked tired, Holly thought, and worried.

'What's wrong with Trog?' Holly asked.

'Pat's not sure,' said her mother, 'but it's probably nothing to worry about. She wants to run some tests.'

'Getting a bit old, like your nana,' Nana Matty smiled.

'You don't do poohs on the floor!' George squealed.

'That's very true,' Nana Matty chuckled. 'But my eyesight definitely isn't what it was, and my poor old legs are getting stiffer by the day.'

'Don't say that, Nana,' Holly protested. 'You're still a spring chicken. Dad's always saying so.'

'Mrs Frillyknickers got deaded by the poxy fox and now she's under the apple tree,' piped up George.

Holly gazed out of the window and saw where the

earth under the apple tree had been disturbed. It was such a tiny patch compared to the mountain of earth that would need to be moved if Finnegan were to have been buried.

'You will help, Nana, with the posters?' she said.

'Yes, Holly, I'll be delighted to help,' Nana Matty smiled.

# Chapter 12

For a moment, when Holly came downstairs the next morning, she couldn't work out what was different. And then she realised that there was no slobbery mouth to greet her, no crusty old paws to stand on her bare feet. Tibbles, stretched out on the comfy chair, raised her head briefly and blinked at her, but promptly rested it again and resumed her snoring.

'Morning, Tibbles,' Holly said, running her hand quickly over the cat's tummy. 'Nice to see you too.'

The doorbell rang and she saw her father move from the back room to answer it. Then, as she took some scrambled egg from the saucepan on the range, she overheard Postman Cyril telling him that he had just delivered a very important-looking letter from the ministry to Councillor Hodson.

'I expect it's the official letter to tell us what they're going to do with the whale,' the postman said.

'I expect you're right,' her father replied. 'Well I, for one, think there's only one place that whale belongs, and that's here on this island.'

'Well, I don't know, John,' the postman said doubtfully. 'I guess it's for them to decide.'

'Rubbish, Cyril,' her father almost shouted. 'They don't bother with every sheep that dies on the island, do they?'

'A sheep's not quite the same as a whale though, is it?' the postman argued.

'It's the same principle. I don't buy into any of this business about it belonging to the Crown. Since when has the Crown had any real interest in our affairs. Anyway, the mainland can't just pick and choose when it feels like it. It can either have all our carcasses – sheep, pigs, cows, seals, chickens, the lot – or none at all.'

That's right, Dad, you tell him, grinned Holly to herself.

'Well I can't see them giving in if that's what they've decided,' Postman Cyril said, pathetically Holly thought.

'This isn't just about what they've decided.' Holly could hear her father beginning to sound exasperated. 'It's about what we want as well. And we're going to start tomorrow night by having a meeting in the village hall to decide what exactly we do want. If you care about this island, Cyril, you'll be there.'

'Oh, I will be there,' the postman said quickly. 'I never said I didn't care, and you know me, I like to keep informed about what's going on.'

'Then, please, while you're on your rounds, see how many other islanders you can inform about the meeting.'

Holly's father closed the door on him and came into the kitchen, just as her mother and George came in from taking scraps to Gerda the pig. 'Some of the people on this island are so spineless,' he hissed. 'They'd rather sit on their backsides and nod their heads dutifully than stand up for what's important.'

'Perhaps they don't think it is important,' said Holly's mother.

'Then they're stupid,' responded Holly, annoyed that her mother was trying to be kind to the enemy again. 'How can anyone not think it's important for us to keep Finnegan?

'I'm just saying that it's not an issue for some people. They don't really care either way. And for others it is an issue because they don't want to keep Finnegan.'

'That's just what Nana said last night, but I bet most people on the island will agree with Dad and me that the skeleton should be kept here,' Holly said defiantly.

'And I agree too,' her mother smiled. 'So you'd better get this petition of yours going, and be prepared for a fight, not just with the mainland but with some of your friends as well.'

'They won't be friends of mine if they don't sign,' Holly scowled. She rushed upstairs to get ready for school. From her desk, she pulled out the sheets of paper that she had ruled up ready for people to sign. SAVE FINNEGAN, each sheet was headed, and underneath it she had written: *We, the undersigned, want the skeleton of our fin whale to stay on our island.* (Her mother had told her to put the 'undersigned' bit.) Her excitement mounted at the thought that at last their battle was about to begin. She signed her name with a flourish in the first ruled column.

'Bye, Mum. Bye, Dad,' she called, as she raced back downstairs again.

'Aren't you going to walk with me and George?' her mother asked.

'Not today, Mum,' Holly replied, going out through the front door. 'I want to get there early to get some names.'

She couldn't believe how cold it was when the morning air wrapped itself round her, so different from the day three weeks before when she had woken to discover Finnegan on the beach. Three weeks of wondering what would happen to him. Now they knew.

'Don't worry, Finnegan,' she murmured to herself, shivering. 'You're staying here with us.'

She spotted Rosie further up the road and called out to her to wait. When she caught up with her, she thrust the petition into her hands and said, 'You can be the second to sign, if you like.'

Rosie looked at the piece of paper. 'Great,' she said. 'If you give me a spare sheet, I'll take it home tonight and get the rest of my family to sign.'

Freddy came up behind them and was about to ask for a sheet for himself when Alice came out of her house just ahead of them. She stopped and waited for them to draw level.

'Daddy's had a letter from the ministry this morning,' she announced importantly.

'We know. Postie told us,' said Holly, and watched the look of displeasure on the Councillor's daughter's face.

'That postman should learn to mind his own business,' she said. 'Anyway, the skeleton is going to be removed from the beach and taken to the heritage museum on the mainland.'

'We know,' said Holly. 'Everybody knows.'

'Guessing's not knowing,' said Alice.

'We guessed right, though,' said Freddy, 'and now we're going to do something about it.'

'You can't do anything about it,' said Alice.

'Would you like to sign our petition?' asked Rosie. 'It's to say that we want our whale to stay here.'

'Daddy says we must do what the ministry says,' Alice said haughtily, 'and anyway, who wants a pile of bones cluttering up our beach?'

'You sound like old Mildew,' said Holly.

'I don't care what you think, Holly Wainwright, and I won't sign your stupid petition and neither will my friends.'

'That's all right,' said Freddy, 'we won't need your signatures. We'll have enough without.'

The three of them picked up speed and left Alice trailing behind them.

Holly was delighted, as they reached the school playground, to see that Mrs Hardaway was on duty and standing on her own.

'You watch this,' she said. 'I'm going to get her to sign.' She left Rosie and Freddy to corner some of their friends, while she approached their teacher.

She was utterly dismayed when Mrs Hardaway explained that she couldn't.

'I'd rather not make my views public by signing your petition,' the teacher said. 'It might upset some of the parents if they think I'm trying to influence the class.' She winked at Holly, then bent down and whispered, 'That doesn't mean that I'm not one hundred per cent behind you, and I'll do everything I can to help save the whale for our island. I just can't sign anything, that's all, and I'd rather you didn't collect names right under my nose.'

'Does that mean we won't be able to do posters in our art class?' Holly asked.

Mrs Hardaway thought for a moment. 'I can't actually set it as a project,' she said carefully, 'but I could invite the class to do posters on whatever subject they like. Then, if some of you choose saving the whale as your topic –'

'Lots of us will,' jumped in Holly.

'I shall be interested to see what you come up with.'

Holly watched her teacher totter off across the playground on her impossibly high heels, and agreed with her father that she was a good sport. She rejoined Freddy and Rosie as the school bell rang and told them that they had their teacher's support but not her signature.

'How many have you got so far?' she asked.

'Only four,' said Rosie. 'It's taking ages because eveyone keeps asking questions. Mary Cooper and a couple of the others won't sign because they reckon we'll get into trouble. Marjorie Daws won't because she says she's sick of the sight of the whale.'

'Some of them say they'll have to ask permission from their mum and dad,' added Freddy. 'Don't worry, though, this is just the start.'

Holly wasn't about to worry. What did she care if a few namby-pamby scaredy-cats didn't want to sign?

Their names wouldn't be missed anyway, especially once people like Big Jim and Peter Marshall and Nana Matty had signed. They were the important ones. If they signed, nearly all of the grown-ups would follow suit.

And then, suddenly, she was hit by another great idea, as they walked through the school door.

'Hey, why don't we get some leaflets printed? Then we can get Cyril to post them to every house on the island when he does his round.'

'Do you think he would?' asked Rosie.

'I bet Dad could persuade him,' said Holly.

'If not, we can cycle round on our bikes,' said Freddy.

Holly whooped at that idea. She skipped into the classroom, plonked herself down on her chair and pushed the petition papers into her desk.

'I hate you, Holly Wainwright,' Alice leant across and hissed. 'You're just trying to make trouble for my daddy. Well, it won't work because nobody important is going to listen to you.'

Holly stuck her fingers in her ears and her tongue out of her mouth, until Mrs Hardaway saw her, then she pretended to be rubbing her ears and licking her lips. She was determined that at lunchtime they would go round everyone in the school and ask them to sign. She was sure Dotty Pinkerton and Ruby Tyler, the dinner ladies, would be on their side.

Dotty Pinkerton was as wide as Ruby Tyler was thin, and as loud and bossy as her friend was quiet and shy. She was popular, though, always ready with a hug and comforting words of advice for anyone, adult or child, who was down in the dumps. If Dotty Pinkerton signed, then Ruby Tyler would surely follow, for they were the best of friends.

The lunch bell having sounded, Holly rushed to the door and across to the canteen. She thrust the petition and a pen under Dotty Pinkerton's nose and begged her to sign.

'Please,' she wheedled. 'We need all the names we can get and it's soooo important.'

Dotty paused and looked at Ruby, while Holly crossed her fingers, then she took the pen and said, 'Good for you, young lady. It's time we stood up for ourselves, and I'll sign for Joe too, to save you the effort of chasing him down.'

She handed the petition to Ruby, who giggled awkwardly, then signed her name with care and gave

128

it back to Holly. 'It's a good idea,' she smiled shyly. 'But I'll leave my husband to sign. He'll want to sign for himself. But he will sign, I know he will.'

'Thank you,' grinned Holly, taking her plate of food and beginning to move away. 'We're going to do some posters as well, and some leaflets,' she said over her shoulder, and instantly regretted it because Marjorie Daws was standing close by. Who cares? she thought. If she tells her mother, the whole island will know very quickly and they'll all be coming to sign.

In the playground, after lunch, Holly, Freddy and Rosie darted around asking their schoolmates to join their campaign. Holly was encouraged by the excitement her petition began to generate and the offers to help from some of the children. It seemed that very few children were talking about anything else by the time the bell went for afternoon classes to begin.

'How many do you think we've got?' she asked Freddy and Rosie as they went back into the building.

'Must be about thirty,' said Freddy.

'There are only about sixty-five children in the school,' said Rosie, 'and some of them are too young to ask.'

Just then, Holly spotted the Head coming out of his office. She hurtled in his direction, waving the petition in the air.

'Sir, sir,' she cried, 'we're doing a petition to save the whale for our island.'

'So Mrs Hardaway tells me,' he said, peering at her over the top of his spectacles. 'It's probably best if not too much activity takes place on the school premises. I wouldn't want Councillor Hodson to think that I am allowing them to be the seat of a revolution.'

Holly wasn't too sure she understood what he was saying, but she nodded her head anyway and turned to walk away in case he decided to tell her off. As she did, he tapped her on the shoulder and said quietly, 'I shall be at the village hall tomorrow night, voting for the whale to stay, of course.'

Holly nodded and felt herself flush with importance. Mr Roger Rowland, the Headmaster, was confiding in Miss Holly Wainwright, a mere schoolgirl! She found it impossible to concentrate for the rest of the day, as she dreamt of her fame spreading across the island. She was a crusader, leading the fight for their survival. She would tie herself to the ferry landing stage and refuse to move until she got her way. She would lead a protest march to the mainland and hurl tomatoes at members of the government if they refused her demands. She would do interviews for the television and then, wherever she went, people would recognise her as the girl who stood up for the rights of a small island. Suddenly, she felt very grown-up and wanted somehow to stay that way.

She came down to earth with a bump when Mrs Hardaway made her stand up and repeat what she had just said – Holly didn't have a clue – and warned that if she didn't pay attention she would stay behind for one of Mr Rowland's punishments. She ignored Alice's titters and put on a studious face for the rest of the day, because she wanted to go home and see Trog. She also wanted to see what was happening on the beach and she had to visit Nana Matty and ask her to start doing posters urgently.

On the way home, Freddy and Rosie agreed to call in on Peter Marshall at the hotel to ask if he would sign the petition and put up a poster. As Holly continued on her own, the first thing she saw was that the bulldozer was installed on the beach and work had begun on removing the fleshy parts from the whale. It was such an unfitting end for such a magnificent creature, to be diced up, thrown into containers and dumped into a landfill site. It made her even more determined that at least Finnegan's skeleton should be given the respect it deserved, and that meant that it should stay as close as possible to its final resting place. She quickened her pace, reluctant to dwell upon what exactly the salvage people were doing, and scrambled down the grassy slope on to the road below outside Lobster Pot Cottage.

Trog's excited bark greeted her as she went through the front door. She scratched his nose when he padded up to her, and she realised how relieved she was that he was all right.

'We got lots of names on the petition, Mum,' she called. 'Even the dinner ladies signed.'

'That's good,' her mother replied.

'Mrs Hardaway can't sign because it might upset some of the parents, but she's on our side.'

'That's good too.'

Holly hoicked Tibbles out of the comfy chair and sat

down. George was out playing somewhere so the house was lovely and peaceful. Trog put his chin on her knee and gazed up at her with milky eyes. She stroked his silky ears. 'Trog seems all right,' she said. 'What did Mrs Roberts say?

'I'm afraid Trog is a rather sick dog,' her mother sighed. 'The truth is, Holly, that he has a growth in his stomach, a nasty one, and that's what's causing his problems.'

'So what's Mrs Roberts going to do about it?' Holly demanded.

'I'm afraid there's not a lot she can do. Trog's too old to undergo treatment.'

'What does that mean then?' Holly could feel herself getting agitated. Trog, sensing it, pined a little.

'It means, my love, that he's not going to get better. It means that he could get worse.'

Holly's eyes began to fill up. Even if her mother wasn't saying the words, Holly knew what she meant.

'But he's not that old,' she protested.

'He is for a dog of his kind,' her mother said gently.

Holly looked at her mother and saw that she was upset as well. Trog had closed his eyes, but his chin was still resting on her leg. 'You'll be all right, won't you, Troggy?' she said. 'We'll look after you.'

'Of course we'll look after him, but there may come a time when it will be kinder to let him go.' Her mother was squeezing her shoulder now.

'Not because of him being a bit sick or doing a pooh in the house,' Holly said hotly.

'Because the time may come when he's in pain,' her mother replied.

Holly didn't want Trog to be in pain. She remembered the time when he trod on a thorn and howled his head off. She remembered when he got a fishbone caught in his throat and couldn't breathe properly. She remembered when he ate a box of chocolates and was sick for days.

'Why does everything have to die?' she murmured.

'It's the penalty we pay for living,' said her mother. 'And Trog's had a good life.'

'Well, he still might get better,' Holly said stubbornly. She wasn't going to give up hope. She made up her mind there and then that she would give him all the love and attention she could, when she wasn't fighting to save Finnegan. She looked at Trog, snoring down by her feet, nose twitching in his dreams. She was only two when her parents had brought him to live with them. It was as though he had been there for ever. She had only known Finnegan for a few hours before he died, and yet she had been so sad and wanted something to remember him by. She had only known Mrs Frillyknickers for a few months, but she missed her frilly walk and her dark brown eggs. What would it feel like if Trog wasn't there any more?

She didn't want to think about it.

When her mother left to collect George, Holly jumped to her feet, checked that there were plenty of biscuits in Trog's bowl, then set off to see Nana Matty. Her grandmother was sitting at her sewing machine in the middle of making a quilt when Holly tapped on the window. Holly felt a stab of impatience that Nana Matty wasn't already working on a poster, especially since she had just received a text message from Freddy saying that Peter Marshall would let them put one up in the hotel.

'Who's the quilt for, Nana?' she asked.

'I promised I'd make one for Margaret Meldrew,' her grandmother replied. 'She gets so cold in that draughty old cottage of hers.'

'Maybe if she had a warmer heart she wouldn't feel the cold so much,' growled Holly, annoyed that Old Ma Meldrew's needs were being put before her whale.

'I'm sure there's a warm heart there somewhere,' Nana Matty said brightly. 'It's just been squeezed into a deep, dark corner. She's not such a bad sort when you get to know her.'

'You're as bad as Mum, always seeing the good in people,' Holly grumbled.

'There's nothing wrong in that, Holly. Anyway, why are you so grumpy?'

'Trog's very ill.'

'Poor Trog, yes. Your mother told me. It doesn't seem five minutes ago that he was gambolling over the rocks like a spring lamb.'

'He was funny when he fell into that rockpool chasing a crab, wasn't he, Nana?' grinned Holly.

'That's better, young lady. I thought you were never going to smile again. Now, how about one of my specials? My poor old fingers need a break from all this sewing.'

'Do you think you could do a poster to go up in the hotel?' Holly asked as her grandmother cut her a huge chunk of fruitcake. 'And do you think you could do it so that it can go up tomorrow before the meeting in the village hall? I want those biologist people from the mainland to see it, and Peter Marshall's given us permission.'

'Goodness me, Holly,' Nana Matty smiled, 'when you get an idea in your head, you're like a terrier gnawing at a bone.'

'But it's urgent, Nana. We want those people to know how we feel, and some of them might be on our side if they know how much it means to us.'

'I hope you're not jumping the gun, Holly. We don't even know for certain how many of the islanders will agree with us.'

'We'll make them agree with us. That's what the meeting tomorrow night is for, isn't it?' Holly said earnestly.

'You can't make people agree, dear,' said Nana Matty patiently. 'You just have to hope that they will when all the arguments are put forward.'

'Well I bet most of them will agree. I've already got lots of names on my petition.'

'And what about poor Margaret Meldrew?' Nana Matty had a twinkle in her eye.

'She won't sign,' Holly said scornfully. 'Not in a zillion years.'

'I meant what about her quilt.'

'It's not cold yet. Please, Nana Matty. You know your posters are better than anyone else's.'

'Flattery, young lady, is a very sneaky means to get your own way.' Nana Matty looked at Holly sternly. 'Now, just you wait here a minute,' she said.

She disappeared out of the room. Holly could hear her shuffling around in a back room and wondered anxiously what she was up to. A few moments later, her grandmother reappeared and waved a large sheet of paper triumphantly in the air.

'You see – you didn't need the flattery,' she chuckled.

Holly stared at the paper. Slap bang in the middle of it, in huge orange letters edged in black, were the words: SAVE OUR WHALE. Swimming through the 'O' was a whale, and in its mouth was a notice which read: 'Keep me on Colmer Island'. The rest of the paper was covered in large waves sweeping on to a beautiful sandy beach, with the sun shining brightly from the top right corner.

'Oh Nana,' cried Holly. 'You're such a star. It's

perfect – better than anyone else could do. You wait till I show my friends.'

'So now can I get on with Margaret's quilt?'

Holly kissed her grandmother on the head. 'If you really can't think of anything better to do,' she said, shaking her head sombrely.

'Holly Wainwright, I should put you over my knee and smack your bottom,' Nana Matty said in mock horror.

'You'll have to catch me first,' Holly grinned. 'Bye, Nana.'

# Chapter 13

At school the next day, everybody was talking about the meeting in the village hall. Some of Holly's classmates were highly indignant because their parents were not allowing them to go. Alice was one of those who had to stay at home, but she pretended that she didn't care since it was all a waste of time.

'The Minister is arriving tomorrow. Daddy says that he will go to the meeting tonight and tell everyone that the decision has been made and that it is final. He says that people can huff and puff all they want, but nothing will change.'

'He's supposed to represent us,' said Freddy. 'If the majority of islanders want the whale to stay, then he's supposed to fight for us, even if he doesn't agree. He should tell the Minister what we think and make him change his mind.'

'He doesn't think that the majority do want the whale to stay. He thinks people are just being emotional at the moment, and that when they see the skeleton they'll think it's an eyesore.'

'Well, if he won't fight for us then we'll have to choose someone who will,' said Holly.

'Like who?' scoffed Alice.

'Like – like Big Jim.'

'Huh! He's just a ferryman,' said Alice.

'And you're just a snob,' retorted Rosie.

Holly chuckled to herself again about how quiet little Rosie burst out of herself every once in a while. It had so much more effect because it was so unexpected. For a brief moment Alice was speechless, then she turned and marched away.

'Nice one, Rosie,' said Freddy.

Holly, Freddy and Rosie were all going to the meeting.

'Just let anyone try and stop me,' said Holly. 'This concerns us as well, not just the adults, and we're the ones who have done all the work so far.' She had got up especially early that morning to take Nana Matty's poster to the hotel, and had been thrilled when Peter Marshall had offered to make some colour photocopies of it so that it could be put in lots of different places. He had hung three in the hotel. After school Holly planned to put one on the door of the village hall, one on the noticeboard by the ferry landing stage and one in the window of Lobster Pot Cottage. Freddy was going to pin one up in his mother's waiting room and he was going to ask Jean Westcott if she would put one up in the pub.

As she left for the village hall with her father that evening, Holly could hardly contain her excitement. She was only sad that her mother couldn't go as well, but she had to stay at home with George.

'What if we need your vote?' she had asked her mother.

'Don't worry. It won't all be over in an evening,' her mother had reassured her.

The light from her father's torch darted animatedly in front of them. Holly was delighted to see other people leaving their cottages and walking in the same direction, and there were more cars on the road than she had ever seen before.

'Will I be allowed to speak?' she asked her father.

'I think perhaps this time you should leave the speaking to the grown-ups,' her father replied, but Holly was determined that, if necessary, if the adults were too namby-pamby, she would stand up and have her say.

'How many people do you think will be there?'

'Half the island, I hope,' her father said. 'Certainly the fishing community all know about it, and most of them are behind us. Joe Pinkerton and Arthur Tyler have spread the word amongst the farmers, and Big Jim has talked to everyone who has taken the ferry over the last couple of days.'

They turned up the road that led round the back of the hotel and onwards to the hall. Just as they did, Peter Marshall and Andy Westcott came out of the hotel and began to walk with them.

'I've left Jean in charge of an empty bar,' Andy Westcott chuckled. 'But we'll all go back there afterwards, if the vote goes our way.'

'It will go our way,' said Holly.

'Where's this petition of yours, then?' he asked.

Holly pulled it from her pocket and handed it to him.

He signed his name and his wife's, and passed it on to Peter Marshall. Holly looked up at her father and grinned.

' "We shall defend our island, whatever the cost may be," ' quoted Peter Marshall as he pointed out that he had already signed. 'You're doing a great job, Holly. We'll need all the support we can get.'

Holly was dismayed to see Old Ma Meldrew plodding along the road ahead of them. She didn't bother to go and see Finnegan while he was alive, Holly thought, but she can be bothered to come up here to get him sent away. She hoped there wouldn't be too many other islanders piling through the doors of the village hall ready to agree with her grumpy old neighbour. Why couldn't she just have stayed at home on her own as usual?

'I hope you're not going to give us any of your tourist attraction nonsense,' she aimed at Peter Marshall as they drew alongside her.

'I'll use every argument I can think of,' the hotel owner replied brightly.

'As for you, John Wainwright, I'm surprised at you, bringing your daughter along to something like this.'

'Holly has as much right to a say as everyone else,' Holly's father replied.

'I don't know what this island's coming to,' the old woman said, and stomped off through the hall doors.

'We're pleased to see you, too,' Andy Westcott fired at her disappearing back. 'Miserable old sow.'

The village hall was so packed that they only just managed to squeeze in at the back. Holly spotted Rosie with her family, and then she saw Freddy and his parents near the front with a spare seat next to them. Her father was already deep in conversation with one of his fishing friends, so she decided to leave him and make her way to the empty seat. As she pushed forward, she was delighted to see Mr Rowland, with his wife on one side and Mrs Hardaway on the other. When the Head acknowledged her with a brief nod, she waved back, thrilled again to be taking part in such a momentous occasion.

She sat down, just as Councillor Hodson made his way up on to the platform followed by Big Jim. A wave of shushes spread round the hall. Councillor Hodson puffed out his chest and looked at his watch. At the back, people were still trying to push their way in, to the annoyance of those who were being squeezed into a smaller and smaller space. Holly spread herself in her seat and whispered to Freddy, 'Most of the island must be here.'

'Shows how important our whale is,' Freddy whispered back.

Councillor Hodson cleared his throat, clapped his hands and asked for silence. The shushes sprayed round the room again, until at last it was quiet.

'Thank you all for coming here tonight,' the Councillor began. 'I hope we can get this business sorted out quickly.'

*This business!* Holly bristled.

'The arrival of a large whale on our island was, I appreciate, an extraordinary event, and we have been privileged to see such a large animal from close up. It was an unhappy circumstance for all of us when the whale died, almost certainly from ill health, so the experts tell us.'

*Circumstance! What sort of a word is that?* Holly looked for Freddy's reaction and saw him pull a face.

'Since then, we have had the rather odious task of

dealing with the whale's remains – which are not, uh, inconsiderable.'

The Councillor seemed to think he was being funny, and looked around for approval. Holly stared witheringly at the one or two people who chuckled.

'I know that some of you would like to keep the whale's skeleton on the island as a sort of – memento. However, I am here to tell you that we can't.'

'Why not?' a voice called out.

'Because it doesn't belong to us,' the Councillor replied firmly.

'Poppycock!' another voice cried. 'You tell us who has more right to it than us.'

'Hear! Hear!' several more voices joined in.

*You tell us*, Holly mouthed.

'It belongs to the Crown, whose officers have decided that it should be housed in the heritage museum on the mainland.' The Councillor had to shout to be heard above the groundswell of anger.

'That's where we disagree.' Big Jim spoke for the first time. 'It may belong to the Crown, but that doesn't prevent it from remaining here, where it was found.'

147

*By me!* Holly sat tall in her seat and wriggled her bottom.

'Hear! Hear!' the voices joined in again, more loudly this time. Holly and Freddy joined in with them.

'We may be a small island, separated from the mainland, but we are governed by the mainland and have to accept many of its dictates, like it or not. In this case, we don't like it and are prepared to fight our corner.' Big Jim paused while the crowd cheered. 'You can argue all you like that the whale belongs to the Crown. That may be correct, but so does this island belong to the Crown. All we are asking is that the whale be left on Crown property here, where it was found, by the sea, rather than in some concrete building in the middle of a city.'

The Councillor puffed out his cheeks as another wave of cheers took the wind out of his sails. He waited until they had subsided, looking round the room to see where his own support might come from.

'You can't just assume that everyone agrees with you,' he said at last. 'Plenty of people I've spoken to do *not* want the eyesore of a whale skeleton cluttering up our village.'

'Hear! Hear!' Old Ma Meldrew rasped.

'The whale is part of our history and we'll all remember the day it landed on our shores,' the Councillor continued, 'but we don't need a physical reminder of it, any more than we do of a dead sheep.'

Someone at the back of the hall booed, and there was a general chorus of disapproval. The Councillor was about to say something else, when Mr Rowland rose from his seat.

'I beg to differ, Councillor Hodson,' he began. 'I think we *do* need a physical reminder. The beaching of the whale was the most momentous thing to happen on our island in many years. For a moment it lit up the lives of our children in a way that made them feel part of something very special. In years to come, they will be able to tell their own children about the day the whale washed up on our shores. And their children will understand more the magnitude of the event when they look at the skeleton and see its sheer size. Pictures in books won't do that for them, and nor will their imaginations, because nobody could ever imagine a creature so vast. So don't talk to me about dead sheep. They are everyday – this is once in the lifetime of a chosen few.'

Holly leapt to her feet. 'Hear! Hear! Mr Rowland, Hear! Hear!' she cried, then sat down and blushed as the islanders applauded.

Big Jim moved centre stage. 'I think it's time we put it to a vote,' he said.

'You can vote all you like,' the Councillor interrupted, 'but it won't make any difference. I have it in writing that the skeleton will go to the museum, and they won't change their minds.'

'We'll see about that,' Holly's father called from the back.

'We will have our vote, come what may,' said Big Jim, 'and if we vote to keep the whale, then we shall expect you, as our representative, to present our wishes in as positive and persuasive a way as possible.'

The Councillor bowed his head for a moment, then drew a deep breath. 'Have it your own way then,' he said. 'I shall, of course, represent the wishes of the majority, to the best of my ability, just as I always have, but I can tell you again that it's a waste of time.'

'Standing up for your rights is never a waste of time,' replied Big Jim, 'even if you lose.'

'We'll vote by a show of hands,' the Councillor said, taking charge again. 'Those who wish the skeleton of the whale to remain on the island, please raise your hands now.'

All round the hall, hands shot up in the air. Holly and Freddy stretched theirs as high as possible and waggled their fingers to make sure they could be seen amongst the forest of arms.

'That's nearly everybody,' Holly whispered to Freddy.

'Looks like it,' said Freddy.

'And now, all those who would rather the whale's skeleton be removed, please raise your hands,' said the Councillor.

Old Ma Meldrew's hand went up straightaway, as did those of Winnie Hodson, Constable McKee, Cyril Blackburn and several others.

'I think that's pretty conclusive,' said Big Jim, after the cheers and whoops and hurrahs had died down.

'It appears so,' Councillor Hodson was forced to

admit. 'Well, all I can do is let the Minister know the result of our vote and see what he says.'

Holly jumped to her feet. 'You can give him our petition,' she said, 'then he'll know that the children want Finnegan to stay as well.' She sat straight back down again, a bit taken aback by her boldness.

'I don't think there'll be any need for that,' the Councillor replied.

'Why not?' Big Jim rounded on him. 'The more ammunition we have, the better.'

'I'm sure the Minister won't want to be bombarded with pieces of paper,' the Councillor argued.

'It's not about what he wants,' Holly's father called out. 'We want him to see the depth of our feeling on this matter, and Holly's petition is a tangible example of that.'

Holly hadn't a clue what 'tangible' meant, but it sounded good and she liked the idea of her petition being an example of it.

'Well, it's up to you if you want to give him your petition,' said the Councillor. 'But I don't think it will make an ounce of difference. Once the mainland has decided something, it rarely changes its mind.'

With that he closed the matter by leaving the platform and heading for the back door. Holly turned to Freddy and shook his hand.

'We won,' she said. 'They can't ignore us now.'

# Chapter 14

The Minister from the mainland arrived the next morning, accompanied by the curator of the heritage museum. They stayed for an hour, chaperoned by Councillor Hodson, then caught the next ferry back. The islanders were furious.

Over supper that evening, Holly's father raged about how little their island seemed to matter.

'He might just as well not have bothered to come at all. He was only concerned about how the stripping of the flesh was going. Big Jim tried to speak to him on the ferry, and all he would say was that he had been made aware of our views and would pass them on to the relevant department.'

'I didn't even have time to give him my petition,' Holly grumbled.

'Don't you worry, Holly,' said her father. 'We'll carry on with your petition until it's got everyone's name on it and then we'll go to the mainland and waggle it under their noses, if necessary. Not only that, but we'll bombard the newspapers and radio and television stations with our protests. This is just the beginning. We're not going to stop at the first hurdle.'

That was what Holly wanted to hear. Her own efforts had only just begun. She didn't want it to be all over yet. And at least Alice hadn't been able to brag about the Minister staying at her house. In fact, she must have felt a bit sick about his whistle-stop visit.

'According to Winnie Hodson,' her mother said, 'the Minister thinks we have little chance of winning because hardly anyone will see the skeleton if it stays here, whereas lots of people will see it in the heritage museum.'

'That's just the point though, isn't it?' her father replied. 'If it's here, it's another thing to attract visitors to the island. It will give us an identity, something to feel proud of. I'm with Peter on this. We need more tourists, and I think we have every right to be selfish.'

Just then, Trog woke suddenly and yelped. He tried

to stand up in his basket, but yelped again and flopped back down. Holly sat on the floor next to him and stroked his ears. He closed his eyes and went back to sleep, but he kept twitching.

'Sleep tight, Troggy,' Holly whispered. 'Just think about those crabs.'

'I don't think he'll be chasing crabs any more, poor old Trog,' her father said.

'It doesn't stop him remembering,' said Holly. 'And in his dreams he can be superdog and catch them all, can't you, Trog?'

'I think we should keep him indoors at night from now on,' her mother said. 'A bit of warmth and comfort won't do any harm.'

Holly's father didn't argue, and Holly knew then that Trog really must be in a bad way. She determined again to give him as much loving as she could to help make him better.

When, in the early hours of the following morning, she heard her father set off on a fishing trip, she got out of bed and pulled on her clothes, even though it was a Saturday. Downstairs, Trog was stationed by the front door, looking abandoned.

'Do not worry, O Defender of the Lobster Pot,' Holly said, patting him on the nose. 'I shall feed you your breakfast and take you for your walk this morning. You won't need to wait while the mistress of the house plays lazybones.'

Trog scratched at the doormat.

'Mr Impatient,' Holly scolded, opening the door.

Trog hobbled out into the grey morning and looked to Holly to show him which way to go. She turned down towards the beach.

'You won't be able to chase crabs or paddle, but you'll be able to feel the sand between your toes,' she said. She noticed how slowly Trog walked now, and that he was panting although they had only just set out. 'We won't go far,' she promised, 'but the fresh air in your lungs will do you good, even if it doesn't smell great at the moment.'

The villagers had grown used to the terrible smells that came from the beach, especially when the wind was blowing inland. They were desperate for the clear-up operation to finish, so that the beach could be restored to them and they could rediscover the joys of watching the waves breaking on the shore, walking by the sea edge and laughing at the seals bobbing up and down. The children had been deprived of their favoured all-in-one football pitch, cricket pitch, volleyball court, climbing apparatus and pebble skimming station, unpopular though they made themselves sometimes when they came down en masse and spoiled other villagers' quiet moments.

As she approached the back of the beach, Holly saw that her own quiet moment was about to be disturbed. Someone was sitting on the wall, a plume of smoke rising from a cigarette. Holly thought about turning back, but she was curious to know who else was up and about this early in the morning. A few steps more and she saw that it was one of the men from the mainland, a biologist or whatever he called himself.

'Morning,' he said. 'You're up early.'

'So are you,' replied Holly, unsure as to whether or not he was an enemy and therefore not worthy of her attention.

'I love it here,' he said. 'It's so peaceful. Just the sound of the sea and the birds waking up —'

'Those pesky gulls, you mean!' Holly corrected him.

'Better than the sound of traffic,' said the man. 'That's what I wake up to at home.'

'There's not much of that here,' said Holly.

'You're lucky.'

Holly stared at him. He was quite young, she thought, for a biologist. Before they had arrived on the island, she had imagined biologists to be old with grey beards, bald heads and spectacles, not that she had imagined them very often.

'Do you like your job?' she asked. 'I mean, it's a bit gruesome, isn't it, cutting up dead animals?'

'It's fascinating, and you get used to the gruesome part. I've never cut up a whale before, though, and none of us has ever had the chance to study a fin whale.'

'What can you tell by cutting it up?' Holly was beginning to be fascinated herself.

'All sorts of things, like what it eats, how it breathes, how it communicates, how it swims, even why it died.'

'It was ill. That's why it died,' said Holly. 'My dog's ill, but I'm giving him lots of love so that he'll live longer. I tried to look after the whale – I was the one who found him you know – but I couldn't do enough for him.'

'I'm sure you did your best,' the man smiled. 'I'm Tom, by the way. Tom Clarkson.'

'I'm Holly,' said Holly shyly, 'Holly Wainwright.'

All of a sudden, she felt close to him, close enough to ask him the question that had been hovering in her mind since they first started speaking. 'We want to keep Finnegan's skeleton on our island,' she blurted out.

'So I heard, and I don't blame you either. Leave it here and it will be part of the museum of island life. The word museum comes from the Greek meaning "home of the Muses". If anywhere should be home of the Muses, this island should.'

Holly gazed at him with awe. *The museum of island life.* What a brilliant expression, she thought. They could use that on their posters, in their leaflets, in their letters to newspapers.

'Will you sign my petition, then, to make the mainland let us keep him?' she asked.

'I'd be delighted to. I'm sure some of my colleagues will as well.'

'Do you think so?' Holly had been so certain that they would all be on the side of the mainland. 'I'll bring it down to you,' she grinned. 'How much longer do you think you'll be here?'

'For ever, if I had my way,' Tom said wistfully.

'We should be through in about four more days. The weather and the sea will finish the job, cleaning the last of the flesh from the bones.'

Holly nodded her head and gazed across the beach at the tarpaulin screening the whale. Then she looked down at Trog, who was resting his chin on Tom's feet, his eyes closed. 'Come on, Trog,' she said. 'Let's go and have breakfast.'

'He's a lucky dog having you to look after him,' smiled Tom. 'My dog would love to live out here with all this space to run around in.'

'Trog can't really run any more,' said Holly, 'but the fresh air will do him good.'

She waved goodbye and began to walk back up the road, before she turned and called, 'You could always come back one day, and bring your dog.'

'You know, I might just do that,' he smiled.

# Chapter 15

The islanders, galvanised into action by the meeting in the village hall and the token visit of the Minister, were only too happy to sign Holly's petition. Some of them even sought her out and took extra pages of it away with them to ask their own friends and family to sign. When at last she had all the names she thought she could possibly collect, she put them into a stamped envelope, addressed to the Minister, and gave it to Postman Cyril.

'You will make sure it doesn't get lost, won't you?' she said. She was unhappy that she had to entrust it to him, because he had refused to sign on the basis that his wife was friends with Councillor Hodson's wife and he didn't want to upset them.

'Well, I'm not going to deliver it personally, you know,' he chortled, 'but I'll make sure it gets on to the ferry, even though I'm not really in agreement with it.'

Holly gave him her most withering look.

Holly's father sent an article about their plight to as many national and local papers as he could find addresses for. DJ Dum and DJ Dee talked about their campaign on the island radio. The island blog was filled with indignant pieces about the 'bullyboy' mainland, though there were also emails from Councillor Hodson and a number of 'anons' who wanted the skeleton removed.

All they could do then was wait.

When the biologists had finished their work, packed their bags and were heading for the ferry, Holly caught up with Tom and thanked him again for his support.

'Good luck with the campaign,' he said, 'and say goodbye to Trog for me.'

'Come back soon,' Holly said shyly.

'Try and stop me,' he grinned.

On the beach, workmen were removing the last of the containers and pulling down the tarpaulins. The villagers began to gather to have a closer look at what it was they were fighting to keep. It was an extraordinary sight, the sheer scale of it astounding the growing crowd.

'That's quite something, isn't it?' Big Jim said to Holly.

'It's awesome,' said Holly.

'Worth fighting for, I reckon.' He winked and strode off up the beach.

As soon as the rope barriers had been taken down, the villagers surged forward, eager to explore and touch the whale's bones before the sea separated them again. Holly moved with them, and then cussed as she heard George's voice shrieking at her to wait for him. She turned as he threw himself at her and nearly bowled her over.

'I want to see,' he cried. 'Lift me up, lift me up.'

'You're too heavy. Wait for Mum.' Holly could see her mother trying to catch up but stuck behind a group of dawdling onlookers.

'Can we go inside it?' George pleaded.

'It's not a Wendy house,' growled Holly.

'It's still got nasty bits stuck all over it,' George said, looking disgusted as he went up close.

'The weather and the sea will clean the last of the flesh from the bones,' Holly said knowledgeably.

Their mother reached them then. 'My goodness,' she said. 'It's just incredible. The jawbones alone must be twelve feet long.'

'They're this long,' cried George, stretching his arms out as wide as they would go. 'And his tail's this long,' he added, trying to stretch his arms out even further.

'They'll need a crane to move it, won't they?' asked Holly.

'They might have to take it apart and put it back together again, if it's going to go to the mainland.'

'Mum!' Holly almost shouted. 'It's not going to the mainland. It's staying here in the museum of island life.'

'I hope you're right, Holly, but I'm just being realistic.'

'Don't be. Be positive like Dad and me. Anyway, Dad says that even if they say no, we're still going to keep it.'

'What's he going to do? Hide it from them?' Holly's mother wasn't being sarcastic in a nasty way. She had a smile on her face, and Holly knew that she was only trying to stop her from raising her hopes too high, but it irritated her nonetheless.

'He'll find a way, Mum,' she said, as her mother set off

165

in pursuit of George, who had by now run round the other side of the skeleton. 'We'll find a way. You wait and see.'

It was only a short time afterwards that the news came through that the islanders' campaign had failed. Arrangements were being made for the skeleton to be removed within the next six weeks. Holly couldn't believe it. All the hard work they had put in and still the authorities on the mainland wouldn't change their mind. How could those people be so stubborn and pig-headed and selfish and unfair? What was worse was that Alice was all full of 'I-told-you-so' and 'Daddy-told-you-so' and 'It's the best thing for our island' and 'Who wants that ugly great thing there anyway?'

And Old Ma Meldrew couldn't resist leaning over the garden gate and saying, 'At last we're going to see the back of that eyesore. Perhaps everyone will come to their senses now and stop all this nonsense about keeping it'.

Holly discovered how fickle people could be, when some of those who had supported the campaign now said that perhaps it would be better if the skeleton were housed somewhere else.

'It's like they've just given up,' she raged at Freddy and Rosie. 'How can they just give up like that?'

But even she didn't really know what else they could do, until her father said, 'Just you wait and see,' and gave her a great wink.

Holly visited Nana Matty and asked her what she thought.

'I'm afraid it's the way of things, dear. The bigger player holds all the trump cards. We can scream and stamp our feet all we like, but if they don't want to listen they can send us away with a pat on the head and there's little we can do.'

'They haven't even patted us on the head,' Holly said grimly. 'They've just said no, and that's it. Well, they won't get away with it because Dad's got a plan.'

'Has he indeed? And what would that be?'

'I don't know. He won't tell me because I'm just a kid. But he's been meeting with Big Jim and Peter Marshall and Mum says they're up to something.'

Nana Matty put a cup of tea and a large slice of lemon drizzle cake in front of her. 'I must say the skeleton is a quite extraordinary sight, especially in the early evening when the sun is going down and its last rays light up the tops of the ribs. It's like a knitting together of nature.'

'It's the museum of island life out there, Nana Matty,' Holly said seriously. 'Did you know that the word museum comes from the Greek meaning "home of the Muses"?'

'Well I never,' exclaimed Nana Matty. 'You do come out with some remarkable things, young lady. Now, how's that young dog of yours?'

'Very sleepy, Nana, and a bit thin because he's not eating enough, but he always sleeps more when it's colder. It'll be better for him when it gets warmer again.'

'You're right. Old bones don't like the idea of winter being on its way. I'd hibernate myself if I could.'

'You're not allowed to, Nana, because we'd miss you too much,' protested Holly.

'I've got far too much to do to hibernate,' Nana Matty laughed. 'Apart from anything else, it's the ceilidh in four weeks' time and I'm in the middle of doing the posters.'

'Whoopee!' cried Holly. 'I'd forgotten all about the ceilidh, what with the whale and Trog.'

'I shall expect a pretty young thing like you to be danced off your feet.'

'You're the one who grabs all the best-looking men,' Holly grinned.

'Old lady's prerogative,' Nana Matty smiled. 'Now off you go and let me get on with my chores.'

Holly kissed her nana goodbye and made her way home. The ceilidh – that was something to look forward to, and then Christmas wasn't long after that. She gazed across the beach at Finnegan's skeleton. What a brilliant Christmas present it would be if he were still there on Christmas morning.

# Chapter 16

Trog was very ill that night, whimpering with pain, Holly's mother told her. Holly had slept through it and was furious with herself for not being there for him. When she went downstairs the next morning he was asleep, but she saw suddenly how very thin he had become.

'Can't we make him eat more?' she asked. 'He must be starving.'

Her mother looked at her quizzically. 'I can't force him to eat if he doesn't want to,' she sighed. 'I'm afraid it's not looking very good for him, love.'

Holly knelt beside him. Hot tears spilled down her cheeks as she stroked his ears. He lifted his head a little and tried to look at her, but the effort was too much and he sank back down on to his blanket. Holly wrapped it round him and was comforted when he wagged his tail. At that moment George came tearing into the kitchen, scattering toy cars all over the floor.

'Take them out,' she yelled at him. 'The last thing Trog needs round him at the moment is you being noisy.'

'Don't take it out on George,' her mother scolded gently. 'He doesn't understand.'

Holly was so angry that Trog was being taken away from her that she wanted to kick something hard and beat her fists. She protested vehemently when her mother said she should get herself ready for school. 'I don't want to go to school,' she howled. 'Trog needs me here with him.'

'Trog needs peace and quiet, and you need to concentrate on your schoolwork, which has been suffering somewhat since the whale came. Honestly, Holly, it's not going to help matters having you mooch round the house all day.'

'I won't mooch. I'll just sit quietly with Trog.'

'No, Holly, now get yourself ready.'

Holly took one last look at Trog and sloped off to get dressed. When Peggy came to collect them because it was raining, Holly bent down and ruffled Trog's head. 'Goodbye, Trog,' she whispered. 'See you later. I love you.'

'Bye, Troggy,' George shouted, as they went through the door. 'I love you too.'

It felt worse than ever being in the car that morning with Marjorie and Bella Daws. Marjorie went on and on about the dress her mother was making her for the ceilidh, and wanted to know what Holly would be wearing. Holly didn't want to think about the ceilidh at that moment. All she wanted to do was think about how she could help to make Trog better when she went home that evening. She was wondering if her mother would let her give him some steak. She was sure Trog would eat steak. After all, it was a real treat when they had it themselves, and her mother was always saying how good it was for them.

She escaped with Freddy as soon as they reached the school. 'Trog's got worse,' she told him, biting her lip. 'I wish your mum could make him better.'

'She can't always,' said Freddy. 'She would if she could.'

'It's just like with Finnegan. I wanted to do something

to help him, but nobody else did.' She knew it wasn't really true, but she wanted someone to blame.

'Finnegan couldn't be saved. You know that.'

'And now they're going to take him away and we'll have nothing left of him.'

'We'll have the memory of the day he landed here.'

'That's not very much,' Holly said hotly. And then, 'Anyway, Dad and Big Jim and Peter Marshall have got a plan to save him.' She wasn't supposed to say anything about it, but she couldn't help herself because she wanted so much to believe that, whatever it was the three men were hatching, it would work, and that somehow Trog's fate was all wrapped up in it. 'Don't tell anyone,' she added quickly.

'What are they going to do?' Freddy was intrigued.

'Dad won't tell me because he says it would be hard for me to keep it a secret, which is so unfair.'

'I'll ask Mum if she knows,' said Freddy.

'She won't tell you if she does,' Holly was sure about that. 'She won't be allowed to tell you if Dad can't tell me.'

Sitting in lessons for the rest of the day was excrutiating. All Holly wanted to do was to go home. When at

173

last the bell went for the end of school, she ran down the road without waiting for her friends.

There was no Trog wagging his tail to greet her when she opened the front door of Lobster Pot Cottage. She went into the kitchen and his basket was empty. Her mother appeared from the garden. Holly saw instantly that her eyes were red and puffy.

'Where's Trog?' she asked.

Her mother came towards her and tried to hold her hand.

'Where's Trog, Mum?' Holly asked again.

Her mother took a deep breath. 'I'm afraid we had to have him put down, Holly.'

Holly stared at her mother in total disbelief. 'Why? Why did you have to have him put down?' she said. She could feel herself panicking.

'He was so ill, Holly, and in so much pain. It would have been unkind to let him go on.'

'He might have got better, Mum,' Holly said, trying to keep control. 'How do you know he wouldn't get better?'

'Because Pat Roberts said so, and because she said that Trog was suffering badly.'

'How does she know?' Holly cried, pushing her

mother's hand away. 'She doesn't know everything, and Trog's not her dog. He's ours and it's up to us not her.'

'I made the decision, with your father. I'm sorry, Holly. I know it's hard, but sometimes you have to be cruel to be kind.'

'You didn't even let me say goodbye to him,' Holly said angrily.

'You gave him lots of love this morning before you went to school.'

'That's not the same, and anyway it didn't work. You should have let me stay home. You should have let me be with him.' Holly was sobbing now, uncontrollably.

'Holly, love, I didn't know it was going to end like this, otherwise I would have let you stay.'

Holly heard the quaver in her mother's voice. She wanted to wrap herself round her, because her mother was as upset as she was, but she couldn't push away the feeling that in the end she had let Trog down and that it was her mother's fault.

She looked at his empty basket, the few biscuits scattered in his bowl and the squidgy toy that he liked to chew on. That was all that was left of him. The realisation that she would never hear his bark, never stroke his silky ears, never run with him across the sand, never chase crabs with him, never see him again, was just too awful. 'I didn't even say goodbye,' she sobbed.

Her father arrived home with George. George ran into the house.

'Mummy, Mummy, Troggy's dead and he's not coming back,' he shrieked.

Holly put her hands over her ears. 'Shut him up, Mum,' she cried.

Her father came and put his arm round her shoulder. 'I know it's a tough one,' he said, 'but it was the best thing for Trog.'

'Why couldn't you have let me see him one more time?' she said.

'He was in a very bad way, Holly. You wouldn't have wanted to see him like that.'

'Bad Trog,' said George.

Holly raised her eyes heavenwards, but didn't say anything. She just wished she could be on her own with her mother and father, to talk about how she felt, to talk about how *they* felt. She didn't want to have to put up with George's shrieks and yells.

She was relieved when, after supper, her mother took him off to bed.

'Were you there when they, you know, when they . . .'

'Put Trog to sleep do you mean?' her father asked.

'He's not asleep though, is he? Why do they say that? If he was asleep, he would wake up.'

'It sounds kinder, less final,' said her father.

'I miss him already,' said Holly. 'I missed him being under the table when we had our supper. I miss him putting his head on my lap. I miss him sitting on my feet.'

'I miss not being able to take him out for his evening walk,' said her father, 'even though it's pouring with rain. I miss his snorts and snores.'

'I miss his farts,' Holly giggled.

'They were awful, weren't they?' her father chuckled.

'Like stink bombs,' Holly hooted. 'But not as bad as Postie's breath.'

'Nothing's as bad as that, poor Cyril.'

'What do you mean "poor Cyril"? He doesn't have to smell it.'

'I s'pose not.' Her father paused for a moment before saying, 'At least he's not suffering any more.'

'Who, Postman Cyril?'

'No, you daft duck. I meant Trog.'

Holly snuggled up to her father. 'What are you going to do about Finnegan?' she asked.

He looked at her long and hard, tweaked her nose playfully, and said, 'We're going to hide him.'

Holly looked at her father in absolute astonishment. 'What do you mean hide him? How can you hide him?'

'Don't ask me anything else,' he said. 'I shouldn't have told you that much.'

'But how can you hide a whale?'

'Just you wait and see, young lady. Just you wait and see. And don't go telling anyone else.'

'Of course I won't, Dad,' said Holly.

# Chapter 17

Breakfast the next morning was a miserable affair. It was so quiet and the kitchen felt so empty. Holly sat down with Tibbles on the comfy chair and tickled her under the neck, until her purr machine sounded as if it might explode. George asked when Trog was coming back and filled his bowl with biscuits in readiness. It was a Saturday, which threatened to hang heavily, because quite often on a Saturday they used to go for a walk together with Trog, who would bound along in front of them.

Holly tried to concentrate her thoughts on the Christmas ceilidh and what she was going to wear. She decided to go and see her grandmother. Nana Matty always made her costume, and anyway she was the sort of person you wanted to see when you were down in the dumps. She set off under a gloomy sky which threatened rain, passed Postman Cyril, who was blowing loudly into a handkerchief but waved as she went by, and found herself catching up with Freddy, who was sauntering towards Peggy Daws's shop.

Holly wasn't sure that she wanted to talk to Freddy. She was still angry that his mother hadn't done more to help Trog. It was too late to walk away though, and in any case she couldn't resist the thought of dropping a few hints about her father's plans for Finnegan. 'If you're after chocolate,' she called out to him, 'I bet it's all gone.'

Freddy turned round and she watched his expression change. 'I'm really sorry about Trog,' he said. 'Mum told me.'

'So am I,' Holly said curtly, to stop herself from crying.

'Mum said there was nothing she could do and that he was in too much pain.'

'He's not any more.' Holly bit her lip.

'Do you remember that time when we took him up into the hills and he saw a rabbit and ran off after it and

180

didn't come back for an hour?' Freddy said, gazing awkwardly at the ground.

'It started to rain and we got wet,' said Holly.

'Wet!' exclaimed Freddy. 'We got soaked to the bone.'

They sat down on the wall at the end of the beach. Finnegan's skeleton stood out eerily against the grey sea. A gull was perched on one of the ribs, pecking away at a tiny morsel of flesh.

'Did I ever tell you about **the** time when Trog raided Mum's handbag because he could smell the chocolate bar she had inside it? She thought we'd been burgled, because everything from her bag was scattered all over the floor, and then she saw Trog with an empty chocolate wrapper.'

'Yeah,' Freddy grinned, 'and that wasn't the only time he stole food. Do you remember that box of chocolates he ate and Mum had to come and check him over?'

'He was a bit naughty sometimes,' said Holly wistfully.

An awkward silence passed between them, and they gazed out across the sand.

'Mum's heard that Finnegan died of a heart attack,' said Freddy at last.

'How can they tell that?' Holly said in amazement.

'Mum said they can tell by the state of the heart, like they can with humans.'

'Finnegan's heart must have been gigantic.'

'Bigger than us probably.'

The two friends sat there wondering.

'You'll never guess what,' said Holly. 'But you've got to promise not to tell anyone.'

'I promise,' said Freddy.

'They're going to hide Finnegan so that the mainland can't have him.'

Holly watched for Freddy's reaction and was delighted by his look of total disbelief.

'You're joking,' he said. 'How are they going to hide something that big?'

'I don't know,' said Holly, staring at Finnegan's skeleton and trying not to doubt it herself. 'Dad just said that they were going to hide it so that the mainland can't have it and that I wasn't to tell anyone. I don't think he'll mind me telling you though,' she added hastily.

'But if they hide it,' said Freddy, 'we won't be able to see it either.'

Holly hadn't thought of that, and she wondered why her father hadn't thought of it either. 'Perhaps they're going to hide it for a while, until everyone gives up looking for it or forgets about it, and then they'll conveniently find it again.'

'It sounds crazy to me.'

Holly looked at him irritably. 'Well, I'm sure Dad knows what he's doing,' she said, before jumping up from the wall and continuing on to Nana Matty's.

Nana Matty was sitting at her sewing machine. She gave Holly a hug when she saw her. 'It's so sad, the news about Trog,' she said. 'How are you feeling, Holly?'

Holly shrugged her shoulders. She didn't know how she felt at that moment. In a small space of time she had been distraught and angry and sad and gloomy, and now she felt sort of empty and just a little bit disbelieving, like Freddy had been over the idea of hiding the whale. She had to keep pushing away the sense that when she went home again, Trog would greet her at the door like he always did. She was also annoyed that her father hadn't confided in her more completely about his plans for saving Finnegan, because then she could have put Freddy right instead of being made to seem foolish.

'I'm OK, sort of,' she said. And then she started sobbing again, just like that, with no warning. She rubbed her eyes angrily with her fist. She didn't want her grandmother to think she was a crybaby.

'It's all right to have a cry,' Nana Matty said. 'It's good to let it out. I wouldn't mind betting that even your mother and father have shed a few tears. And you've had a lot to cope with, what with all the ups and downs over the whale.'

'And Mrs Frillyknickers,' sniffed Holly. 'I keep thinking I'm all right, Nana, and then I start off again.'

'It'll take time to come to terms with losing Trog. He was a big part of the family – like another brother or sister.'

'Better than George,' muttered Holly.

'Holly!'

'Sorry, Nana, but he's just really, really annoying sometimes, and he keeps asking when Trog's coming back.'

'Poor wee thing doesn't understand, but he'll be just as upset as you are in his own way.'

Holly wasn't sure she wanted to think about George being upset. It was bad enough having to deal with her own feelings, let alone worry about her brother, and anyway he seemed more puzzled than upset.

'Dad's got a plan to hide Finnegan,' she said, eager to change the subject, but then she wished she hadn't because that was the second person she had told and she wasn't supposed to tell anyone. She hoped that Nana Matty didn't really count because she was family.

'I know,' said Nana Matty. 'And I don't think you're supposed to be telling anyone, are you?' She looked questioningly at Holly.

Holly turned away and fiddled with the material in the sewing machine. 'I thought it would be all right to tell you,' she muttered.

'As long as you don't tell anyone else,' Nana Matty warned. 'It could spoil everything.'

'I won't,' said Holly. She quickly changed the subject. 'What do you think I should wear to the ceilidh, Nana?'

'What sort of thing do you want to wear?'

'I thought I might wear a dress this time, instead of dungarees,' Holly said tentatively. She had in mind a bright red dress, in fact, with a big swirly skirt that would fly in the air when her partner spun her round, but she didn't really want to say so in case her grandmother thought she was silly.

'A dress would be nice,' Nana Matty smiled at her. 'A pretty one with a big swirly skirt to show off those long legs of yours.'

'Red, I thought,' Holly said, blushing. 'Red with shiny bits.'

'I'll see what I can rustle up.'

'Let's not tell anyone,' Holly urged, 'then they'll all be surprised to see that I'm not wearing trousers.'

'My lips are sealed,' said Nana Matty, 'so it's up to you, Holly.'

'I won't say a word to anyone about anything,' promised Holly.

# Chapter 18

The days began to grow shorter and colder. By half past three in the afternoon, it was dark. Finnegan's skeleton seemed to shrink into itself as the wind swept the sand in blizzards across the beach. Trog's absence from the cosy kitchen of Lobster Pot Cottage, especially first thing in the morning and in the evening during supper, was like a wound that would seem to be mending but then opened up again. Holly couldn't get used to the empty space in front of the range. George had finally stopped asking when Trog was coming back, but not before he had thrown tantrums and howled and sobbed in turns. Even Tibbles had seemed lost without her clumsy friend. She had sniffed all round the kitchen over and over again, and searched the gardens and his kennel.

At school, the conversation was all about the ceilidh and who was wearing what and who was going to dance with whom. Holly kept saying that she didn't know what she was going to wear, more because she had begun to worry that everyone would look at her if she appeared in a dress than anything else.

'You'll be the belle of the ball in this,' Nana Matty had said when she had shown her a deep red shiny material with a thin gold stripe through it.

It was exactly what Holly had dreamt of, but when her grandmother added that she would have all the young men falling at her feet, she had felt herself blush redder than the material, and wished that she could go in dungarees after all. She liked the idea, though, of being asked to dance by Freddy or Peter Marshall or one of Rosie's brothers, and when Nana Matty brought the dress to the house for her to try on, she suddenly felt very excited. She stood in front of the mirror and twisted her hips from side to side. The dress swirled round her in a big undulating circle, revealing a swish of petticoat underneath and quite a lot of pink leg. She giggled with delight.

'I'll knock everyone over with this,' she said.

'You'll bowl them over you mean,' smiled her

mother. 'I didn't realise my daughter was growing up so fast. You're turning into a proper little lady.'

Holly's excitement was ruined when, a few days before the ceilidh, Alice announced that Finnegan's skeleton would be removed two days after the event. 'Daddy's had a letter saying that they want to take the skeleton away before winter sets in properly, and the beach is going to be closed off again so that the workmen can dismantle it without any interference.'

'Dismantle it?' said Holly. 'What do they mean "dismantle" it?'

'Take it to pieces,' Freddy replied. 'Mum said they would have to do that because it's too big to move in one piece without damaging it.'

'And it won't fit on the ferry in one piece,' said Alice.

'Big Jim might refuse to have it on the ferry at all,' said Holly. 'Especially since he wants it to stay here.'

'It's not up to him,' argued Alice. 'He'll have to do as he's told.'

'How do you know the whale will be there when they come to fetch it?' Holly said, and instantly wished that sometimes she could stop herself from saying what

189

she was thinking, especially when Freddy scowled at her.

'I mean, a great big wave might sweep it away,' she added lamely.

'What are you talking about, Holly Wainwright?' scoffed Alice. 'If it's still on the beach after three months, it's not suddenly going to disappear in the next few days.'

Holly was itching to say, 'You never know,' but this time she managed to bite her tongue. Instead, she ran home that afternoon and accosted her father as soon as he came through the door.

'Finnegan's skeleton is being dismantled two days after the ceilidh. I thought you said we were going to hide it.'

'And I thought we were going to keep quiet about it,' her father said, a warning note in his voice.

'But there's not very long now,' Holly said, desperate to alert her father to the seriousness of the situation.

'We know what we're doing, Holly.'

'Why can't you tell me?' Holly pressed her father.

'Because the fewer people who know, the better.'

Holly's father closed the subject and went outside to lock up the henhouse.

'Anyone would think I was just a kid,' Holly grumbled to her mother. She dug Tibbles out of the comfy chair, sat down with her on her lap and stretched her feet out towards the range. 'Are we going to get another dog?' she asked suddenly. She didn't know where the question had come from, nor whether she even wanted another dog, but the space in front of the range was looking very empty again. Perhaps it was because she had pictured the beach without Finnegan. He had been there so long now that she couldn't imagine what it would be like if he disappeared.

'I'm sure we will, in time,' said her mother. 'It's not something to be rushed though.'

'It's not the same without Trog,' Holly said, stroking Tibbles's ears.

'No, it isn't, is it?' her mother replied. 'I even miss the times when he was a pain in the butt.'

'What, like when he dug up your seeds to bury his bone?' grinned Holly. 'And you went bananas because it had taken you hours to sow them.'

'There'll never be another Trog,' smiled her mother. 'Trog was a one-off.'

'A bit like me,' Holly chuckled.

'One of you is certainly quite enough,' her mother teased. 'Anyway, let's get the winter over and then perhaps we can start thinking about a puppy.' She pressed her finger against her lips as Holly's father and George came back into the house.

Holly ran up to her bedroom. If she kept out of her father's way, she wouldn't keep wanting to ask him what he was going to do with Finnegan and when. She liked the idea of having a puppy. A puppy would be completely different from the Trog she had spent most of her life with, and she had no memory of him as a little Trog. She wondered how Tibbles would react to a puppy, now that she had become the unchallenged Monarch of the Lobster Pot.

'I don't think you'll like it, Tibs,' she said out loud. 'He'll probably make a lot of noise and jump on you and steal the comfy chair.'

She stood in front of the mirror and pulled a face. 'You're growing up, young lady,' she pronounced, 'and things are changing all around you.' She decided to try out new hairstyles to go with her dress for the ceilidh. She lifted her hair and tied it into a ponytail (too sophisticated), then into bunches (too little girly), then into plaits (too serious), until, finally, she scrunched it up wildly, let it drop all round her face, and growled at the mirror: 'I'm Holly Wainwright, the ceilidh queen.'

# Chapter 19

The Christmas ceilidh always took place in Joe Pinker-ton's Big Old Barn. In the days leading up to it, the villagers hung multi-coloured lights and decorations from the rafters and laid bales of straw for sitting on. At the back of the barn, they put in place a makeshift bar, which they stocked high with drinks of all shapes and sizes – some of them homemade and guaranteed to turn your brains into mashed potato and your legs to jelly, Holly's mother said. Next to it, they set up tables for food. Though most of the villagers would eat before they arrived, the night was long and hunger pangs would set in well before the end. In the front corner of the barn, they built a platform upon which the Hooley Stompers would strut their stuff, while next to it they erected tables from which DJ Dum and DJ Dee would operate their sound and lighting equipment.

From seven o'clock onwards on the evening of the ceilidh, front doors began to open and the villagers spilled out on to the roads as though responding to an air raid siren or earthquake warning. No one ever drove, even if it was pouring with rain, because the walking to and from the ceilidh was part of the fun. The walking home was also part of the sobering up for those who over-indulged on the homemade concoctions, even if they did have to be helped to stay on their feet.

Holly was so excited that when her mother let her borrow her mascara, she poked it in her eye and tears rolled down her face for the next five minutes. George kept running round the house yelling, 'The ceilidh, the ceilidh, we're go-wing to the ceilidh.' Her father had been on the telephone behind the closed door of his office for what seemed like hours. Holly thought perhaps he was hiding from her, because he still hadn't hidden Finnegan. 'There are only two days left,' she had said to him accusingly that morning, but all he had replied was that two days was a long time.

Now, at last, they were leaving the house to join the chattering groups making their way to the Big Old Barn. Holly swung her hips and felt her dress struggling to escape from the confines of her coat. Her father put his arm through hers. She decided to forgive him, at least for that evening, for his refusal to share his secret with her. George raced ahead when he saw two of his friends, while her mother waited for Miss Marigold to emerge from her cottage.

'Will you allow me the pleasure of at least one dance with my daughter?' her father asked.

'What's it worth?' said Holly.

'The joy of being in the arms of the most handsome man in the room,' her father grinned.

'Peter Marshall's better looking, and so's Freddy, and so are the DJs,' Holly scoffed.

'Oh, you know how to wound a man. I shall just have to bury myself in a corner and sob.'

'One dance then, but I shall have to share myself out.'

'And this is the girl who refused to come out of her dungarees at the last ceilidh, and tried to avoid dancing with anyone over thirteen. How things can change in just twelve short months.'

Holly squeezed her father's arm to stop him from letting go. She was still nervous about how everyone would react when they saw her dress. Part of her wanted to go home and change, but she grew more confident as the barn came into sight, and especially when Rosie caught up with them and grabbed her other arm.

'You didn't chicken out then,' Rosie giggled. 'I thought you might wind up going in dungarees again.'

'Course not,' said Holly. 'They're for kids.'

Big Jim strode up and Holly's father moved away with him.

'Watch out for your toes if you dance with Big Jim,' Holly chuckled.

'What's happening about Finnegan?' Rosie whispered. 'I thought you said they were going to hide him.'

'Dad won't tell me, but he says they've still got two days.'

'One day,' giggled Rosie. 'Nobody does anything the day after the ceilidh.'

They reached the end of the queue at the door of the Big Old Barn. Freddy was a few places in front with his parents. When he turned round, Holly was amazed to see that he was wearing a dinner jacket and bow tie, even if it was with his customary jeans.

'Look at Freddy,' she nudged Rosie.

'Wow! Bags I get the first dance with him,' said Rosie.

'I'll fight you for it,' grinned Holly.

The queue moved slowly forwards, until at last they spilled into the barn. Holly loved that moment. It was like going into an exotic palace. The rafter lights carpeted the grey stone walls and concrete floor with riots of colour, and disguised the bales of straw as ample plush-covered thrones. Soft music from the DJs' turn-table wove its way round the groups of villagers, as they pressed animatedly across the floor in search of friends and that special place to commandeer for the evening. Holly pushed Rosie forwards towards an empty bale near the DJs. 'We'll be able to see everything from there, and we can tell your brothers if we don't like the music,' she said.

Holly was glad that, even with the lights, it was fairly dark. Rosie was already taking off her coat, to reveal a rather prim pale blue dress that made her look as if she didn't know how to have fun. Holly wondered why

Rosie's brothers, who were wearing brightly coloured waistcoats and bow ties, couldn't have persuaded her to put on something a bit more fashionable. She realised, too, that it was partly because she didn't want all the attention focused on herself. She took a deep breath and undid the buttons of her coat. As she did, she saw Nana Matty come through the door, followed by Old Ma Meldrew. She was so shocked that she didn't even notice her coat fall from her shoulders on to the bale of straw.

'What's Mildew doing here?' she gasped.

Holly wasn't the only one to look towards the door in total astonishment. The whole of the barn seemed to fall silent. Nana Matty greeted everyone with a wave of the hand. Old Ma Meldrew growled, 'What are you all gawping at?' and disappeared into the shadows.

'Nana must be seriously off her trolley to bring that old battleaxe with her,' she said to Freddy, who had come to join them.

'Bit of a surprise,' he said. 'So's the dress. Looks good.'

'But she'll spoil it for people if she sits there looking all grumpy,' Holly continued, and was glad again for the dark, which meant that Freddy couldn't see her blush.

'I wonder why she's come,' said Rosie. 'She's always gone on about the ceilidh being evil.'

Holly watched her nana go up to the bar, order two drinks and disappear in the direction Old Ma Meldrew had taken. 'Nana Matty's even bought her a drink,' she spluttered, 'and I don't think it was water.'

'The next thing we know she'll be asking you for a dance, Freddy,' Rosie chuckled.

Holly laughed out loud. 'That would be worth watching,' she said.

Just at that moment, DJ Dee's voice broke through the music, welcomed everyone to the ceilidh, urged them all to let down their hair, hoick up their trousers, throw up their skirts, and hit the dance floor running.

'Are we going to have a good time?' yelled DJ Dum.

'Yeeeesssss!' cried the villagers.

'Are we ready to begin?' yelled DJ Dee.

'Yeeeesssss!' cried the villagers.

'Then let's hear it for the HOOLEY STOMPERS!' yelled the DJs Dum and Dee in unison.

'Hooray!' cried the villagers.

The Hooley Stompers leapt on to the stage, whooping like a troupe of gibbons. Their leader wrapped himself round his microphone, told the crowd what a fantastic evening they were about to have, and implored them to take their partners for the first dance. Holly turned in Freddy's direction as everyone swarmed into the middle of the floor, but Freddy had already grabbed hold of Rosie. Then she saw Peter Marshall striding towards her, hand outstretched.

'May I have the honour of leading the prettiest girl in the room on to the dance floor?' he said with mock formality.

Holly looked round to see who was watching, before she shyly took his hand and followed him.

'That's a spectacular dress,' he grinned. 'I'm surprised your father let you out in it.'

'Nana Matty made it,' Holly said, and wondered if her grandmother would manage to get Old Ma Meldrew up on to the floor.

'Ah, yes, I must book my slot with that nimble-fingered young lady before I'm too late.'

The opening bars of music started up and DJ Dee called for the dancers to prepare themselves for a do-si-do. Everyone in the room knew what to do, even George, because they went to the ceilidh almost as soon as they could walk. The evening always began with dances that encouraged the participants to mix up and change partners. After that, while some of the villagers became mellow with drink, others cranked up their engines ready for the jives and jitterbugs that would inevitably follow. And, finally, the whole pace would slow, partners would be rediscovered, and the evening would close with sentimental songs that clouded the eyes of the old and embarrassed the young.

Peter Marshall was a good dancer and definitely very good looking, Holly thought, even if he had turned thirty and was therefore pretty old. He twirled her this way and that, and she loved the feeling of her dress swirling round her. When they passed by Alice, who was twisting clumsily in the arms of Alfie Perkins, she leant her head on Peter's arm and felt deliciously smug. She was amused then to see that her father was dancing with Mrs Hardaway, who was wearing a very tight, very short, yellow satin dress that threatened to squeeze her pips out, and she looked as if she had been at the strawberry jam instead of the marmalade. Holly turned her head this way and that in time with the music until she caught sight of her mother, who was clasped tight in

Postman Cyril's embrace. How could she? Holly wondered. She'll keel over. Big Jim hurtled by, partnered by Peggy Daws. She was as round as he was tall but her feet seemed scarcely to touch the ground.

There was no sign of Nana Matty, and Holly was worried that Old Ma Meldrew would spoil her evening for her.

'Why do you think Old Ma Meldrew's come?' she aimed at Peter's ear. The music was so loud that she had to repeat her question but, before he could answer, the rhythm changed and Alfie Perkins grabbed her for the next dance.

'You look all sort of grown-up,' he said, as he took hold of her awkwardly round the waist and trod on her toe.

You look all little boy, she thought to herself, wishing she had seen him coming and ducked out of the way. Luckily, though, it was a dance where you moved from one partner to another round the room. She soon passed on to Danny Perkins, then Mr Rowland, who said she was quite the young lady, then Curly Lockett, and on to Freddy. She decided then that Freddy was the best-looking male in the room and hoped, when he moved on to Marjorie Daws that the music would last long enough for him to come round to her a second time. It didn't, but the Hooley Stompers invited the dancers to take partners again, before they would pause to let them catch their breath. Holly was about to head across the room in Freddy's direction, when her father took her by the shoulder.

'You cannot escape from me, O Daughter of Mine. This dance has my name written on it,' he said.

'I might refuse to dance with you unless you tell me what's happening to Finnegan,' Holly threatened haughtily.

'You don't give up, do you, Holly? Just watch this space, that's all.'

'What's that supposed to mean?' Holly said in exasperation as her father began to spin her round.

'Things might happen sooner than you expect.' He grinned down at her. 'Have you seen who's just taken to the floor?'

She gazed round as Big Jim trotted up behind her, Old Ma Meldrew in his arms. Her mouth fell open at the sight of the ferryman, head held high, smiling broadly, with the old woman, stony-faced, trying to keep a distance between them.

'Why did she come, Dad?'

'Perhaps she was given no choice.'

The music became so loud that Holly couldn't make herself heard to find out who had given Old Ma Meldrew no choice. Her father whirled her round the room at breakneck speed, until she felt quite giddy. She was glad when the final notes sounded, and then laughed out loud when she saw Big Jim bend over in the most exaggerated bow to his partner. She even thought she saw Old Ma Meldrew smile briefly before shuffling back to the shadows. George came rushing over and demanded that his father buy him an ice cream, just as she was going to ask about the old woman again. Her father gave her money to buy a drink and, as luck would have it, she arrived at the bar at the same time as Nana Matty.

'You look stunning, Holly,' her grandmother smiled.

'Thanks to you, Nana.' Holly leant towards her. 'Why did Old Ma Meldrew come?' she hissed.

'I told her she had to or her quilt might disappear in someone else's direction,' Nana Matty chuckled. 'Her cottage really is very cold.'

'But why?' Holly asked. 'Why did you want her to come?'

'Because it's time she learnt to have a bit of fun.'

'As long as she doesn't spoil it for everyone else,' Holly said. 'I can't believe you persuaded her.'

'Oh, I can be very persuasive when I put my mind to it,' Nana Matty said.

'Did you see her with Big Jim?' Holly giggled. 'She looked as if she'd swallowed a lemon.'

'Believe me, she enjoyed every minute of it, which is what I am going to do as soon as the band comes back on. Just watch out, Peter Marshall.' Nana Matty chuckled loudly and disappeared through the crowd.

Holly decided to forget all about Old Ma Meldrew and Finnegan for the rest of the evening. She made her way back across the room, snaking her hips to avoid the dancers who were gyrating to the DJs' disco, and sat down with Freddy, Rosie and Alfie. Nobody was talking very much. The music was too loud, and there was something mesmerising about the movements of the dancers through the flashing lights. Holly caught sight of George wriggling around as though he had ants in his pants before galloping off across the floor and back again. Two or three other children of the same age were prancing around in similar lunatic fashion, as were several children from her own class. She sniffed disdainfully and smoothed her dress down in front of her, then scanned the room to see who she might dance with when the Hooley Stompers began their next set.

She noticed Big Jim, Peter Marshall and her father deep in conversation by the barn doors and wondered what they were talking about. Her mother was close by with Patricia Roberts and Mr Rowland. Gossip, gossip, gossip, Holly thought to herself, switching her gaze back to the dance floor just as the band bounced back on to the stage. To her horror, she saw Postman Cyril heading purposefully in her direction when the instruction to take partners boomed through the microphone. She turned to Freddy to save her, but he had been grabbed by Alice and was already being dragged from his seat. How dare she, he's *my* friend, Holly raged to herself, but it was too late to save herself from the postman's clutches.

'Pillarbox red,' he chuckled, 'what an appropriate colour for a postman's partner.'

'It's cherry red,' Holly argued.

'Close enough,' said the postman.

And you're too close, Holly thought. She turned her head to the side and tried to put as much distance as possible between them, in which ambition she was thwarted by the postman's bulbous stomach. As they blundered round the dance floor, Holly searched desperately for someone to rescue her. She mouthed 'help' at her mother, who shimmied comfortably by in the arms of Mr Rowland and gave her a sympathetic smile. Luckily, the music changed suddenly, which gave Holly a chance to escape using the excuse that there were lots of other people she had promised to dance with. She darted away before he had a chance to argue, and hid behind Betty Lockett and Jean Westcott, who were discussing their husbands' bad habits.

Just then, Dotty Pinkerton barged on to the floor with Big Jim. They began to perform their own chaotic version of the jive, with arms rotating, bottoms bumping, heads wagging and loud hoots of merriment, which brought tears of laughter to the eyes of the onlookers. George, on seeing them, tried to boomsa-daisy with anyone he could, which led to a riot of bumping bottoms from one end of the Big Old Barn to the other. The madder it became, the more the DJs pumped up the volume and the more the Hooley Stompers accelerated the stomp. Holly threw herself into the middle of it, joined by Freddy and Rosie and a dozen of her classmates. There was always a moment like this in the ceilidh when everyone let go of their inhibitions and took off with the music into a frenzy of exuberance.

Nobody could resist the pulsating beat, even Old Ma Meldrew. Holly howled when she saw Nana Matty heading for the floor with the old woman in tow. 'Look!' she screamed at Freddy. 'Mildew's on her way.' She had never seen anything like it. The old woman actually had a smile on her face and her hips were trying to swing.

'She's been at the cider,' Freddy laughed, attempting to breakdance and landing on his belly.

Holly launched herself even more purposefully into her own dance. Partners weren't needed any more. Everybody was dancing with everybody. Some bobbed up and down on the spot, some spun and cavorted all the way round the edge of the floor, some twisted sinuously in and out of the others. Very few villagers sat out now, but those who did wore expressions of the greatest bemusement at the bedlam taking place in front of their eyes. Holly began to giggle as the music reached a crescendo, the beat becoming faster and faster until, with a final crash, bang, wallop of the drums and a cry of 'Thank you!' from the lead singer, it stopped.

Many of the dancers, hot and exhausted, lurched towards the bar and the bales for refreshment and a rest. Others found themselves partners, as the Hooley Stompers played a medley of quieter songs. It was time for Ruby Tyler to emerge from the shadows in her husband's supportive arms. Holly watched in wonder as the shy dinner lady metamorphosed into a lissom dancing queen.

'You wouldn't believe it was the same person, would you?' she said.

'She's like a flower that needs the sun in order to blossom,' said Rosie.

Holly gazed at her friend and added, 'A flower that opens just once a year.'

Nana Matty waltzed past in the arms of Danny Perkins and smiled at her. Holly waved back, before searching the barn for the rest of her family. Her father wasn't dancing and she couldn't see him at the bar either. Then she realised that Big Jim and Peter Marshall seemed to have disappeared as well. She noticed her mother sitting on a bale of straw, George slewed across her lap, apparently asleep, and went over to her.

'Where's Dad?' she asked.

'Having a drink, I expect,' her mother replied, without looking round for him.

'He's not at the bar,' Holly said.

'He's probably gone outside for a chat.'

'Have you seen Ruby dancing? She's like a flower that needs the sun in order to blossom.'

Holly's mother looked at her curiously. 'That's a very grown-up observation,' she smiled.

'I *am* very grown up,' said Holly, straightening her dress a little. 'More grown up than Piggy Hodson, I would say.' She pointed towards some bales where the Councillor was sitting, leaning backwards with his eyes closed and his mouth wide open. 'It's past his bedtime,' she laughed. 'I bet he snores like a Gloucester Old Spot.'

'The poor man has had a very trying time recently,' said her mother.

'He's not the only one,' protested Holly. 'Anyway,

where is Dad? I still can't see him, and I can't see Big Jim or Peter Marshall either.'

'Holly, just get back to your friends and forget about where your father might be, will you?' her mother said. There was a note of warning in her voice.

Holly glared at her. 'You know, don't you? You know where he is and you're not telling me.'

'I know and I'm not telling you, you're right. I'm not telling you because it's important to keep it quiet.'

'They've gone to hide Finnegan, haven't they?' cried Holly.

George stirred on his mother's lap.

'Shhh, Holly, before everyone else finds out.'

'Why couldn't he tell me?' Holly sulked. 'Finnegan's my whale and nobody tells me what's happening.'

'Now you're being childish,' her mother reproached. 'If you really want to do something useful, go and help Nana Matty keep Margaret Meldrew here for a while longer.'

Holly stared at her mother incredulously. 'Why would I want her to stay?' she scoffed.

'Because we don't want her seeing or hearing something she shouldn't.'

Holly stood there frowning, until at last she understood what her mother was telling her, then she felt even more angry. 'Nana Matty knows as well, doesn't she? That's how you got Mildew out of the way.'

'Your grandmother can be very persuasive, especially when she has one of her quilts as a bargaining tool,' her mother smiled.

Holly couldn't believe that her parents and her grandmother had been keeping things secret from her. 'It's so unfair,' she fired.

She stomped off across the room.

'It's tonight,' she said to Freddy, without even stopping to think.

'What's tonight?' he asked.

'They're hiding Finnegan tonight and they've been keeping it a secret from us.'

'It's Piggy and Mildew they're keeping it a secret from.'

Holly looked sharply at her friend. 'Did you know?' she challenged.

'Mum let slip something and I worked it out,' Freddy said carefully.

Holly stared at him with her mouth agape. She felt

her blood boil at the knowledge that even her best friend knew more than she did, and that his mother was in on the secret as well. 'I can't believe you didn't tell me,' she hissed.

'I promised I wouldn't,' Freddy said simply. 'And now I'm going to do something I never dreamt I would.' He nodded towards the barn doors, where Nana Matty was talking to Old Ma Meldrew, who had her hat on and was preparing to leave.

Holly watched as Freddy headed across the floor. The band was playing the opening bars of a ballad, and couples were heading on to the dance floor clutching hands. When he reached Old Ma Meldrew, Holly saw him bow stiffly, the old woman shake her head, Nana Matty remove her hat, the old woman appear to give in, and Freddy usher her forwards.

'Freddy must be mad!' Rosie ran over and grabbed her arm. 'Have you seen who he's dancing with? Everyone's in stitches and Alfie Perkins nearly wet himself.'

Holly grinned in spite of herself. 'Freddy's doing it to save Finnegan.'

'What!' exclaimed Rosie. 'I wouldn't go *that* far.'

'*I* would,' snorted Holly. 'And, when this dance has finished, I'm going to talk to Mildew and say how pleased we are that she came and what a good dancer she is.'

To her immense relief, she didn't need to. The DJs announced that the Hooley Stompers were about to play their final number. They introduced the band members one by one and asked that everyone give each of them an enormous cheer. Nobody wanted the evening to end. Those who had been sitting out suddenly sprang to life again and rushed to join in. George charged across the floor and grabbed Holly by the legs. 'Twist me round,' he cried. 'Twist me round.' Holly looked at her little brother's eager face and laughed. She hoicked him up in the air and spun round with him as the Hooley Stompers belted out their last song. 'Faster,' he screamed. 'Faster.' She twirled faster still, her dress flying high in the air, until she had made herself so giddy that she lost her balance and they fell in a heap on the ground, knocking someone else over with them.

'Silly Holly,' George giggled.

Holly looked round to see Alice on the ground behind her.

'Some people never grow up,' Alice hissed.

'Some people are born ancient,' Holly replied haughtily. 'And some people are going to have a surprise in the morning.'

# Chapter 20

It was a buoyant crowd that toddled tipsily along the road from the Big Old Barn towards the village. There was no moon to brighten their way, just a joggle of torchlights playing backwards and forwards, to and fro. Holly was longing to go down to the beach, but her mother insisted that she go straight home to bed. There had been no further sign of her father, nor of Big Jim and Peter Marshall. Scarcely anyone had commented upon their absence, which made Holly suspicious that more people than she knew about were involved in the plot. She hoped that when they reached the bend in the road she would be able to see if anything was happening on the beach, but it was so dark that she couldn't even tell if Finnegan's skeleton was there or not.

Tiredness had set in amongst the revellers before they reached Lobster Pot Cottage, and all that could be heard up and down the road was the scrape of shoes on tarmac. Holly, George and their mother caught up with Nana Matty and Old Ma Meldrew, who were being escorted home by the Locketts. Nana Matty still managed a cheery 'Goodnight, sleep tight', but Old Ma Meldrew's only response to Holly's mother's 'I hope you enjoyed yourself, Margaret' was to grunt 'A lot of fuss about nothing in my view.'

Everyone slept late the next morning. With no Trog to demand breakfast, and no school or work, it was mid-morning in Lobster Pot Cottage before anyone stirred – apart from Tibbles, who got up from the comfy chair every so often to see if her bowl had miraculously filled up, and then went back to sleep disappointed each time. A loud knocking on the door finally broke through the snorts and grunts and wheezes coming from upstairs. Holly heard her father stumbling along the landing and down the stairs. She heard the front door open and a voice bellowing, 'What have you done with it, hmmm?'

'Morning, Reg,' her father yawned. 'Brilliant night last night.'

'Never mind all that,' the Councillor snapped. 'What have you done with the skeleton?'

'Why, what's happened to it?'

'You know very well what's happened to it.'

Holly leapt out of her bed and ran to the window. She pulled back the curtains, expecting to see an empty beach. It wasn't empty at all. Finnegan's skeleton was still there, a number of villagers standing close by.

'What *has* happened to it, Reg?' her father asked.

'You've stolen its head!' the Councillor spluttered.

Holly screwed up her eyes and looked again. It was true. The main part of the skeleton was still there, but the jawbones had gone.

'I want to know where you've put it,' the Councillor ordered.

'I'll just see if it's somehow slipped into the house.'

Holly giggled as she heard her father scuttle around in the kitchen then return to the front door.'

'It doesn't seem to be here,' he said.

'Very funny,' Councillor Hodson growled. 'You and

**219**

your friends are behaving as if this is some sort of kids' game.'

'And you're behaving like a pompous, self-important old windbag,' said Holly's father.

Even Holly winced at that. She heard her mother hurrying downstairs.

'Now then, you two, what's going on?' her mother said firmly.

'Your husband has stolen the head of the whale,' Councillor Hodson almost squealed.

'Well, I don't think I would have put it quite like that, but, yes, he is responsible for its disappearance. However, I won't stand by and let him call you names, Reg, so I apologise on his behalf.'

'No you don't,' said Holly's father crossly. 'I meant what I said, and if he thinks that anyone will tell him where the head is hidden, he's mistaken.'

'Well, then, you'll have to suffer the consequences,' the Councillor blustered.

'Which will be?' her father asked.

There was no reply and the door closed. Holly skipped downstairs and threw her arms round her father. 'Well done, Dad – that showed him,' she said.

'We don't need to make an enemy of him though, do we?' said her mother.

'He's the one who makes enemies,' retorted Holly. 'Anyway, Dad, where have you hidden it?'

'Under an awful lot of sand,' grinned her father, 'not too far away.'

'But it can't stay hidden, can it?' Holly reasoned.

'It can stay there until the mainland gives up on it and turns its attention to other matters. And if it doesn't give up, then at least it's not having things all its own way.'

'If it doesn't give up, then we'll have to think up a new plan,' said Holly brightly.

Her parents looked at her and raised their eyes heavenwards.

'Sometimes, Holly,' said her mother, 'even the most determined individuals need to accept when they are beaten.'

Holly pulled a face. 'We'll never be beaten,' she said.

A succession of callers that day praised Holly's father and his cohorts for their audacity. Word had spread that Finnegan's jawbones had been hidden under the sand on one of the nearby beaches, but few people knew exactly where, and those who did were not telling. Most of the islanders seemed tickled by the daring of it all, and saving Finnegan was again the topic of conversation wherever groups of people got together. Councillor Hodson and Constable McKee went from villager to villager trying to find information about the missing jawbones, but nobody said a word. Even Old Ma Meldrew seemed to be rather amused at what had happened.

'If I hadn't been at that nonsense in the barn,' she said to Holly's mother, 'no doubt I would have heard or seen something and been able to spill the beans. As it is, I don't know anything, though if it were me, I would have hidden it in a barn over the other side of the island.'

When the experts from the heritage museum arrived the next day to begin work on dismantling the skeleton, they were horrified to find that a substantial part of it was missing. Holly was furious that she had to go to school and so wasn't there to witness their reaction.

'I bet they couldn't believe their eyes,' she said to Big Jim when she and Freddy went down to the beach in the afternoon.

'They were a bit taken aback,' he replied. 'They said they would be reporting the matter to the authorities on the mainland, but would expect us to see sense and return the jawbones forthwith.'

Work continued for several days on the remainder of the skeleton. Little by little it was taken apart, labelled, put into crates and ferried over to the mainland. The inquisition carried on daily as well, Councillor Hodson and Constable McKee asking the same questions over and over again in the hope that someone would give in and tell them what they wanted to know. No one told them anything.

At last, the spot where Finnegan had spent his final hours lay empty. The salvage team departed with the remaining available pieces of their precious cargo, leaving nothing more than a mess of footprints, tyre marks and scrapings in the sand. Waves trickled in and licked these gently away, before the full force of the winter tide wiped out every trace of Finnegan's existence. When Holly, Freddy and Rosie went down to the beach the following morning, they were shocked to see how barren it looked.

'He'd become such a part of the landscape,' said Freddy as they stood where Finnegan had been.

'It's as if we've lost a bit of ourselves,' Rosie mused.

Holly looked at her and nodded wisely, before joking, 'Finnegan's certainly lost a bit of himself.'

'About four metres,' Freddy chuckled.

The three friends laughed and scuffed their way along the sand, arm in arm against the force of the wind. Ahead of them, crabs scuttled into their holes as soon as they felt threatened.

'Trog would have been after them,' said Holly.

'Did he ever catch a crab?' asked Rosie.

'Once,' grinned Holly, 'and then he was so surprised that he dropped it and it ran away again.'

'He was a bit of a nutter,' said Freddy.

'I wish he was with us now,' said Holly.

'Just as well he's not,' Freddy laughed. 'He'd probably have dug Finnegan's bones up by now.'

'Do you know exactly where they are yet?' asked Rosie.

It was the question everybody wanted an answer to. Gradually, stories were being spread that they were round the other side of the island, that they were in one of the farmers' barns, that they were right next to where Finnegan had been lying, but deep under the sand. The villagers all knew that it had taken a chainsaw and a digger to perform the disappearing trick, because Big Jim, Peter Marshall, Holly's father and several other helpers had been happy to enlighten them with an account of their night-time's activities.

'I heard Dad telling Mum that they're by the sand dunes on the next beach,' Freddy said.

'My dad won't tell me anything,' grumbled Holly. 'It's as if he doesn't trust me to keep quiet.'

'Why don't we go and have a look?' said Rosie.

'I'll race you there,' yelled Freddy.

They hurtled off across the sand. Freddy reached the dunes before either Holly or Rosie had even scrambled over the last of the rocks that separated one beach from the other. He was already bent double probing for clues when they ran up to him.

'Can't see anything,' he said.

'The tide's probably washed any clues away,' said Rosie.

'If any part of the jawbones wasn't buried deeply enough, it might be showing by now,' Freddy countered.

They searched over a wide area, but didn't find anything unusual apart from an old sock and a dead crab. The wind bit more deeply.

'If it's here, they did a good job of burying it,' Rosie chattered through her teeth.

'Nobody's going to find it now that winter's here,' said Freddy.

# Chapter 21

It was Marjorie Daws who made the discovery, or at least it was the Daws family's terrier, one afternoon a few weeks after Christmas. Marjorie's punishment from her father for answering back once too often was to take Bingo for a walk. As soon as he was freed from his lead, the dog raced off across the sand, over the rocks and on to the neighbouring beach, where there were rabbit holes in the dunes. Marjorie took her time catching up with him. She was in a sulk at having to go out in the bitterly cold wind, and didn't really care if he disappeared for good. He rushed up and down the dunes, stopping every so often to yap at a hole, before tearing off again like a turbo-charged floormop. She hunched her shoulders, pulled her scarf further round her ears, stuffed her hands in her pockets and cursed.

It was only when Bingo bit into something and started to pull at it, growling furiously, that Marjorie paid him any attention.

'Drop it, Bingo,' she said sharply. 'Drop it now.'

Bingo ignored her and carried on pulling, his tail wild with determination, his growls becoming more and more frustrated.

'Leave it alone, Bingo, for goodness' sake,' Marjorie shouted, then muttered, 'Stupid dog,' under her breath. She wanted to go home now and was irritated that Bingo had chosen that moment to be stubborn. She called him to heel, but he completely ignored her. Finally, she went over to see what he was so excited about.

'It's only some old bone,' she groaned. 'We've got millions of those at home.'

She was about to pick Bingo up, when she noticed that this wasn't just some old bone. From what she could see of the bit that Bingo had his teeth embedded in, it was an unusual shape and there was a lot more of it underneath the sand than was sticking out. It didn't take her very long to gasp in astonishment, push some more of the sand away, then hare back across the beach towards her mother's shop.

'Mum,' she yelled, 'come quickly! I think I've found the whale bones.'

'Shhh,' warned her mother. 'Don't tell everyone.'

Marjorie stopped in her tracks. 'But don't you want to know where they are?' she asked petulantly.

'I know where they are, more or less,' said Peggy, 'and if they're showing I shall get on to Big Jim right away so that he can cover them up again.'

'You never told me you knew where they were,' Marjorie complained.

'The fewer people who know, the better,' Peggy said brightly. 'What have you done with Bingo?'

'He's chewing on the biggest bone he's ever found in his life,' said Marjorie sarcastically. She was angry that her 'find' had been treated with such a lack of appreciation, and she certainly didn't care whether or not it meant that the mystery of the jawbones' whereabouts had come to an end. Her mother, though, sent her father out to bring the dog back, then ran to the telephone and spoke urgently to Big Jim.

'I'm sick of hearing about the stupid whale,' Marjorie said sourly when her mother had finished the call. 'It's so

229

boring.' She went out of the house with her mother's warning not to say anything ringing in her ears.

She didn't really mean to say anything when she met up with Alice and they went to listen to music at her friend's house. Alice just happened to mention that her father was being pestered by the museum about whether he had made any progress.

'He's in such a foul mood all the time because of it,' Alice said. 'He says everyone's made him look a fool.'

Marjorie didn't particularly like Alice's father, but she liked her status as friend of the daughter of the most important man in the village. She also liked the idea of knowing something that would make her even more popular with the Councillor's daughter, as well as making the Councillor himself very grateful to her. In addition, knowing the answer to the island's mystery had already begun to gnaw away at her and she was desperate to share it. And so, as they sat in Alice's bedroom talking about this and that, Marjorie suddenly blurted out, 'I know where the jawbones are.'

She watched her friend's face as she took the information in.

'Where?' cried Alice, looking incredulous. 'Daddy will be so relieved.'

The minute she said it, Marjorie realised that she might become a heroine to Alice and her father, but the rest of the village would hate her, and her mother would be livid. 'Can we just keep it between you and me?' she said lamely.

'Don't be daft,' said Alice. 'It's your duty to tell me, and it's my duty to tell my father.'

Marjorie shifted uncomfortably on the bed. 'I don't want to tell you now. I'll get into trouble. I shouldn't have said anything.'

'If you don't tell me, then I shall fetch Daddy and he'll make you tell him,' Alice threatened. Then she softened her voice and said, 'Look, nobody needs to know that it was you who told us, not if you don't want them to, but you might get into terrible trouble with Constable McKee if she thinks you're hiding something.'

Marjorie glared at her friend, but she was in too far now and she knew there was no going back. 'They're by the sand dunes on the next beach, but you're not to tell anyone I told you,' she muttered.

Alice didn't bother to reply. She ran downstairs to tell

the Councillor. Within seconds he was on the telephone to the curator of the heritage museum. Marjorie hovered at the top of the stairs and wondered if she should make a quick dash from the house. She hadn't liked being threatened by Alice, and she wasn't sure she wanted to be the Hodsons' heroine any more either. It was too late, though. Councillor Hodson spotted her and signalled to her to come down. He finished his conversation with the curator, then turned to her and patted her on the shoulder.

'Well done, young lady,' he said. 'You did the right thing. This nonsense over the whale has gone on long enough and you've done well to put an end to it.'

Marjorie gazed in horror at his smug face and wanted the ground to swallow her up. 'I'd better go now,' she said. 'My tea will be ready.' She made for the door, Alice in pursuit. 'Promise you won't tell anyone that it was me,' she hissed at her friend.

'Of course I won't,' said Alice. 'What do you take me for?'

Once outside, Marjorie was shocked to see that her passage from the Councillor's house to her own was blocked by Big Jim, Peter Marshall and John

Wainwright. She flushed with guilt, and prayed that they hadn't seen her leaving the enemy camp. She hurried along the road, head down, and managed to pass by the three men without being waylaid, only to enter her mother's shop and come face to face with Holly and Freddy. Both of them looked up and nodded at her, then continued their conversation with her mother.

'If it wasn't Bingo, somebody else's dog would have discovered them eventually,' she was saying. 'It could easily have been your Trog, if he had still been alive, Holly.'

'At least it's nearly dark, and Big Jim will be able to get the digger and cover them up before anyone else spots them,' said Holly quickly. She didn't want anyone suggesting that Trog might have given the game away. 'I'm amazed we didn't find them when we were looking round the dunes the other day, unless the tide's uncovered them since.'

Marjorie was dumbfounded that her mother appeared to have told Holly and Freddy all about Bingo's discovery. 'Why did you tell them, Mum?' she snapped. 'It's supposed to be a big secret.'

'You don't think we would give it away, do you?'

Holly jumped in. 'We're the ones who've been campaigning to keep him.'

'Mum said the fewer people who knew, the better,' said Marjorie.

'As long as it's not the wrong people,' Freddy said firmly.

Marjorie felt herself flushing again. 'The wrong people are bound to find out in the end,' she said. 'You can't keep a secret for ever.'

# Chapter 22

Everyone knew the secret was out when, three days later, a team arrived from the mainland together with lifting equipment and a huge container. Councillor Hodson met them off the ferry, accompanied by Constable McKee, who warned the onlooking villagers that there would be no interference or else.

'The jawbones will be restored to their rightful owner,' announced the Councillor, 'and will be displayed for the greater benefit of the nation as a whole.'

'Thanks to Marjorie,' Alice whispered to Holly.

'What do you mean?' Holly hissed.

'She did the right thing by telling Daddy that she'd found the bones.'

Holly was speechless. She ran over to where Freddy

was standing with Rosie. 'You'll never believe it,' she spluttered. 'It was Marjorie who told Piggy.'

'I guessed as much,' said Freddy. 'She was bound to tell Alice about her find.'

'I can't believe she did that when her mum's on our side,' Holly cried. 'Now we'll be left with nothing and it's all her fault.'

'She's hiding. Perhaps she doesn't feel very good about it herself now.' Rosie pointed up at the window above Peggy Daws's shop. Marjorie was standing there watching what was happening.

'Serves her right,' said Holly. 'Traitor. I'm never going to speak to her again.'

They trailed round to the other beach when eventually all the equipment had been offloaded from the ferry. Big Jim pointed to where the bones were buried, under instruction from Constable McKee, and the excavation began. The crowd looked on in silence as the deep covering of sand was gradually removed and Finnegan's nose was revealed. There was a cry of anger then from Holly's father.

'What right have these people to take our whale away? It should have stayed here where it belongs.'

With that, he stalked off across the sand, unable to watch any longer. Holly moved to go after him, but her mother took hold of her arm.

'Let him be, Holly. He needs to be on his own.'

'Is this the end then?' Holly asked.

'There's not a lot more we can do,' she replied. 'There are only so many times you can bang your head against a brick wall.'

'But it's so unfair,' Holly cried. 'Why won't they listen to us?' She could feel the sadness welling up inside her, sadness not just for the whale that had landed on their beach and died there, but for Trog who would never chase another crab across the sand, and even for Mrs Frillyknickers whose skedaddling days were over. There was nothing left of any of them now, just memories that dimmed with every passing day. She had put all her hopes into saving Finnegan. It had given her something to hold on to, something tangible to fight for and, if they had won, his skeleton would have been a daily reminder not just of the most amazing few hours of her life, but of everything she cared for.

# Chapter 23

The removal of Finnegan's skeleton left the islanders bitter and angry. For many of them he had become a symbol of their freedom to decide their own fate, but that freedom had been snatched from them once again. Councillor Hodson was ostracised, and it was some time before Holly and her friends would speak to Marjorie Daws. Gradually, though, as everyone battened down for the winter and the beach became a wild and lonely place, conversations turned away from Finnegan and on to the cost of fuel, the state of the roads, the need for a new church roof, and the news that Constable McKee had accepted a post on the mainland.

Holly hated the long winter days. At least when Trog

was alive there had been a reason to brave the squally winds, because it had been worth it just to watch him chasing after leaves that he could never catch. Now, when she came in from school, she disappeared up to her bedroom to avoid George's chatter, but it was too cold to stay long. Sometimes she gazed out of her window and pretended that Finnegan was still there waiting for the sea to come and fetch him, and that she would sit astride him until a huge wave came and carried them away.

'It's so boring now,' she complained to her mother. 'There's nothing to do since they took our whale.'

'There's just as much to do as there ever was before the whale came,' her mother replied. 'You've got out of the habit, that's all.'

'When I'm old enough, I'm going to leave this island for ever,' Holly said.

'There's no guaranteeing you'll be less bored anywhere else,' her mother replied.

Whenever she could, Holly spent her time with Nana Matty. She loved sitting in her cosy little cottage in front of her big open fire. Her grandmother was making her a new quilt. She was thrilled when she arrived one bright winter morning to find her hard at work on the central panel. The picture taking shape was just like the one on the poster she had painted for saving Finnegan. Holly looked at the tiny stitches round the whale's eye, which was bright and alive.

'That's brilliant, Nana,' she cried. 'You're so clever.'

'I still have one or two skills,' grinned Nana Matty.

And then she showed Holly another part of the quilt that she hadn't seen before. It was only a tiny section, but there was a dog that looked just like Trog, sitting proudly with a crab in his mouth. Pecking at the ground by the side of him was a hen with a frilly bottom, just like Mrs Frillyknickers. Holly shrieked with delight and threw her arms round her grand-mother's neck.

'Steady on,' the old lady gasped. 'I'd quite like to see the arrival of the spring, especially since that's when work will begin on the new entrance to the ferry landing.'

'I didn't know we were having a new entrance to the ferry landing.'

'Neither did anyone else until today,' said Nana Matty. 'Peggy Daws rushed over with the news as soon as she heard it from Winnie Hodson. It looks like your campaign has had some effect after all.'

Holly hadn't a clue what she meant. 'Will you stop talking in riddles, Nana?' she pleaded. 'What news and what campaign?'

'How many campaigns have you conducted over the last few months?' Nana Matty smiled mischievously.

'Do you mean saving Finnegan?'

'We're to have a replica of his jawbones at the entrance. It seems the local authority have been persuaded that they should leave us with something to mark the occasion of his landing.'

'What's a replica?' Holly asked suspiciously.

'It's an exact copy,' Nana Matty explained, 'and it will be made out of stone or something.'

'But that's not the same as the real thing,' Holly protested.

'It's as close as we can get, and it means that the real skeleton will be protected from the elements while we benefit from having a perfect reproduction in place. They do the same thing in art galleries, you know. They keep some original paintings in a vault where they are safe, and hang copies on the walls.'

Holly thought about this for a few moments.

'What persuaded them?' Holly was eager to know all of a sudden.

'Your petition played a big part, and the lengths we were prepared to go to to keep the skeleton here.'

'So it wasn't all a waste of time,' said Holly.

'Even if this hadn't happened, it wouldn't have been a waste of time,' said Nana Matty. 'If you believe in something so strongly, then it's important to make your voice heard.'

'I'm going to make my voice heard now,' laughed Holly.

She kissed her grandmother on the head and ran to the door. She couldn't wait to tell her family and friends and anyone else she bumped into. She wasn't prepared, though, when the first person she saw was Old Ma Meldrew. She wanted to cross the road and pretend that she hadn't noticed her, but the old woman spoke first.

'You look jolly pleased with yourself, young lady,' she said.

'I've just heard some good news,' said Holly.

'Lucky you,' said Old Ma Meldrew. She stood there as though waiting for more.

'We're to have a replica of the whale's jawbones at the ferry landing,' Holly said almost defiantly. She waited for the old woman's biting tongue to make mincemeat of the notion.

'Are we indeed?' Old Ma Meldrew replied. And then, as she continued in the direction of Nana Matty's house, she turned and said, 'I shall look forward to that. Yes, I shall look forward to that.'

Holly gazed in astonishment at her disappearing back. It wasn't just those faraway people on the mainland who had been affected by the campaign. It seemed that even Old Ma Meldrew had had a change of heart. Holly ran on down the road. At the edge of the beach, she stopped and gazed out across the sea. A shaft of sunlight was playing on the top of the waves. For a moment Holly thought she could see a large creature gliding along. She screwed her eyes up, but there was nothing there. She remembered the morning when she had woken up and looked out of her window to see Finnegan lying on the sand like a displaced rock. She remembered looking back at Lobster Pot Cottage to see Trog at the gate. It seemed so long ago, and so much had happened since.

But now she found herself looking forward. Spring was just round the corner. The tree in the garden would soon be covered with frilly blossom. Work would begin on the replica of Finnegan. And the empty place in front of the kitchen range would be taken up by a puppy. Holly thought she heard it barking already and smiled. Then she heard a more persistent barking and turned to find Tom Clarkson walking towards her.

'I said I'd come back and bring my dog with me,' he said.

'I thought you'd come in the summer,' said Holly.

'I couldn't wait that long, and neither could Tiff by the looks of it.'

Tom's dog was already haring across the sand, the wind tugging at his ears. Every time he saw a crab he hurtled after it, then stopped and looked puzzled when it disappeared down a hole. Holly laughed as she remembered the same look of puzzlement on Trog's face.

'We saved Finnegan, you know,' she said.

'The ferryman told me. Good on you. I'll be back in the summer to see it.'

'You can't keep away, can you?' grinned Holly.

'I could be happy here,' said Tom.

'Like me,' Holly smiled.

## Sally Grindley

Sally Grindley lives in Cheltenham and has worked in children's books all her career – first as an editor for a children's book club and then as a full-time writer. Sally is the author of many outstanding books for young readers. She is the winner of a Smarties Prize gold award for *Spilled Water*. Sally travels extensively to research her novels. Her other novels for Bloomsbury include *Feather Wars* and *Hurricane Wills*.

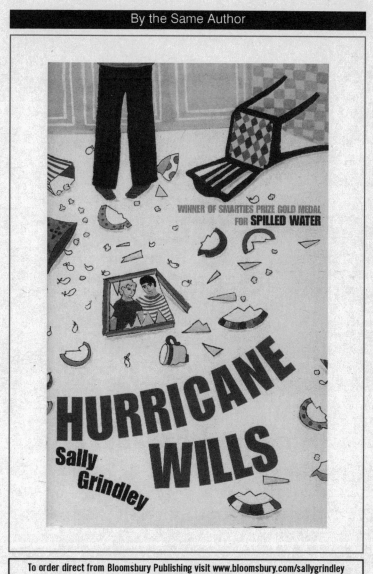

WINNER OF SMARTIES PRIZE GOLD MEDAL
FOR **SPILLED WATER**

HURRICANE
WILLS

**Sally
Grindley**

To order direct from Bloomsbury Publishing visit www.bloomsbury.com/sallygrindley
or call 020 7440 2475

BLOOMSBURY

www.bloomsbury.com

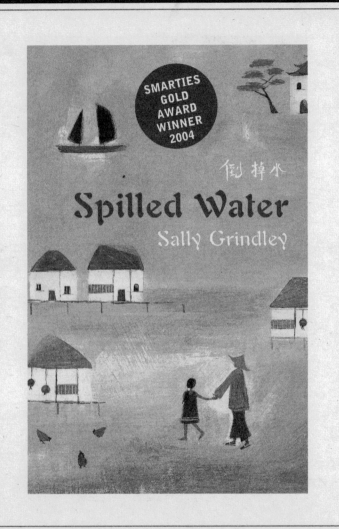

To order direct from Bloomsbury Publishing visit www.bloomsbury.com/sallygrindley
or call 020 7440 2475

**BLOOMSBURY**

www.bloomsbury.com